HOME AT LAST

When Hannah loses her job, house, and professional reputation after unwittingly getting embroiled in a financial scandal, inheriting Rose Cottage seems a blessing. But her plans to quickly sell up stall as her childhood memories of the cottage and her beloved aunt bubble up to the surface, and soon she begins to imagine starting a new life in the little Cornwall village. She also realizes she's falling for her half-Danish, half-American neighbour, Jake the Rake — who turns out to be deserving of his nickname . . .

Books by Angela Britnell
in the Linford Romance Library:

HUSHED WORDS
FLAMES THAT MELT
SICILIAN ESCAPE
CALIFORNIA DREAMING
A SMOKY MOUNTAIN CHRISTMAS
ENDLESS LOVE

ANGELA BRITNELL

HOME
AT LAST

Complete and Unabridged

LINFORD
Leicester

First published in Great Britain in 2015

First Linford Edition
published 2017

A catalogue record for this book is available
from the British Library.

ISBN 978–1–4448–3125–2

Published by
F. A. Thorpe (Publishing)
Anstey, Leicestershire

Set by Words & Graphics Ltd.
Anstey, Leicestershire
Printed and bound in Great Britain by
T. J. International Ltd., Padstow, Cornwall

This book is printed on acid-free paper

1

Whoever named Rose Cottage had a strange sense of humour. Hannah's heart sank as she stared at the house, instantly depressed by the stark granite walls, narrow windows and peeling grey paint. After losing her own house in Watford to the bank, it'd seemed little short of a miracle to inherit this place — but now she wasn't so sure. There was a garden, if you could dignify the jungle she'd waded through from the gate with such a name, but there was no sign any roses ever framed the door. Her childhood memories had let her down big-time.

Hannah reluctantly fished out her phone from her pocket and called her mother. A few creative explanations would be necessary to stop Janie jumping in her car and heading down the motorway to deepest, darkest Cornwall. 'I'm here.' She made an effort to sound bright and cheerful.

'Good. How long do you think it'll take to get ready to sell?'

About a century? 'Not sure, Mum. I'll give you a better idea in the morning when it's daylight.' *Which I'll probably see easily, judging by the blue tarp covering half the roof.* 'I'll talk to you tomorrow.' She hung up before her mother could ask any more awkward questions.

In the historical romances she loved to read, the men always girded their loins before going into battle. Hannah wasn't quite sure if women could do the same, but if it *was* physically possible, now was the time. She stared down at the heavy bronze key in her hand.

'Putting it in the lock usually works, sweetheart.'

Hannah gasped and spun around to face a massive man looming over her with enough blond hair and muscles to suggest a Viking warrior off to do battle. 'Do you usually creep around this way?' she snapped. 'You scared the life out of me.'

His ice-blue eyes swept appreciatively down over her. 'For someone dead, you sound kinda lively to me, sugar.'

She pulled her short black trench coat in around herself and glared back at him. 'I don't know who you are, but you're trespassing on private property.'

'I could say the same right back at you, honey,' he drawled. 'Unless you're my new neighbour, that is?'

'Neighbour?'

'Yeah, I live over there.' He pointed back across the wilderness to another ugly house that must have been designed by the same bad-tempered builder.

'But you're American.'

'We are sometimes allowed to live outside the confines of the United States, you know,' he tossed right back at her. 'Plus, strictly speaking, I'm half-American and half-Danish. Does that make it more permissible?'

She'd been rude, but Hannah wasn't in the mood to apologize. The man stuck out his hand and out of instinct she took hold of it. His grasp was firm and warm, and he held on a couple of seconds longer than polite before she tugged it away.

'Jake Walton. And before you say anything, I don't have a million siblings who are always disgustingly cheerful and shout good night to each other like idiots.'

'What on earth are you talking about?'

He shoved a hand up through his shaggy mess of white-blond curls and cracked a wide smile, a very tempting one she'd bet had lured more than one gullible female. 'I guess you're too young, or too English.'

Hannah didn't respond right away. Nobody had called her too anything in a long time.

'There was a dumb TV programme back in the dark ages that's still being shown in reruns with a sickly-sweet country family called the Waltons,' he started to explain. 'They lived in a big house, and the show always ended with them shouting good night to each other from their bedrooms. Made me want to smack them,' he said with a deep, booming laugh, and Hannah couldn't help giggling.

'It sounds frightful.'

4

'Yeah, it was,' he said and scrutinized her some more. 'Anyway, have we established yet who you are?'

'I know who I am. Would you care to?' Hannah said with a teasing lilt to her voice. Instantly she regretted it when Jake's jaw set in a firm line and his eyes darkened, sending a shiver running right through her.

'Oh, I know who you are now, sweetheart,' he responded with another tempting smile. 'Hannah Green. Mrs. Trudgeon described you perfectly.'

'But I hadn't seen Aunt Betsy in years,' she protested.

'Yeah, I heard.'

Her cheeks flamed at the disdain running through his voice. 'There were very good reasons for that. Private ones that don't concern you,' Hannah made herself clear. 'Now you've established I'm not trying to break in, I suggest you return to your own house and allow me to get settled in here.'

'You can't stay in there tonight,' he said forcefully, and folded his arms across his massive chest.

'I most certainly intend to, so I suggest you mind your own business.'

His warm, rumbling laugh took her by surprise. 'Get down off your high horse, honey,' Jake teased. 'The electricity and water have both been turned off, and you won't be able to get them reconnected until at least tomorrow.'

A wave of tiredness swept through Hannah. 'I'll drive back down into the village and get a room at one of the pubs.'

'You could stay with me,' Jake threw out, and Hannah's jaw dropped.

'You can't be serious.'

'Hey, I'm only offering you my spare bedroom for the night.' His voice hummed with amusement, and another unwanted rush of heat lit up her face.

'So I would assume, Mr. Walton.' Hannah's best haughty manner usually put men in their place, but Jake's expression didn't change. 'Thank you for the offer, but . . . ' A few drops of rain plopped on her head, and a loud crack of thunder boomed as a bright flash of lightening lit up the grey sky. Hannah screamed and threw herself at Jake. She bumped up against his broad chest and through her panic registered his strong arms wrapping around her.

'It's okay, honey.' His soothing voice eased her illogical fear back to something almost bearable. 'We're goin' inside my place. No arguing.'

'My bags.' She attempted a feeble protest and shivered as icy rain pelted down, soaking her to the skin. Out of the blue, Jake swept her up off her feet and into his arms before she could object.

'I'll come back for them,' he said.

'Put me down. I'm perfectly capable of walking.' Hannah struggled in his grasp, but it was like trying to get out of a steel vice.

'You'll slip on the mossy stones in those flimsy apologies for shoes.'

She didn't bother trying to explain they were high-end designer sandals. Judging by his own wardrobe of jeans so worn they had more holes than denim, a faded red flannel shirt and heavy work boots, fashion and Mr. Jake Walton were not best friends.

Hannah slumped in his arms and gave in. For now.

★ ★ ★

Jake left his unexpected guest in the house without saying another word and returned to get her luggage. For a few moments he stood outside the door and let the rain cool him down.

Darn woman. First she pinned him down with those cool sea-green eyes, and then turned small and fragile in his arms. Everything about Hannah Green was refined, from her porcelain skin to the pale gold hair wrapped in an elegant chignon and a voice that could etch glass. He should have paid more attention when Betsy Trudgeon spoke about her niece.

He quickly ran back next door, picked up her suitcases and then trudged back to his side of the hedge. He shoved open the door with his foot. 'Okay, here we go.' The words died in his throat at the sight of Hannah curled up in the corner of his worn black leather sofa, fast asleep.

'Sorry,' she murmured and stirred, stretching her arms over her head and tightening her white silk top around curves he'd have preferred not to notice. 'I must have dropped off.'

The sudden softness in her voice rattled him. Cool and prickly was easier to deal with. 'I'll stick the kettle on,' he offered.

'For an American, you sounded very comfortable saying that,' Hannah teased, and Jake relaxed. Sarcastic humour he could do.

'I'm fixing coffee for myself. Are you satisfied I fit your stereotype now?' he challenged, and she swept her penetrating gaze over him again but held her tongue. He took a wild guess that didn't happen often. 'How do you take your tea?'

'Who's stereotyping now? I hate tea.'

'Won't they strip you of your British citizenship if they find out?' he pushed right back at her.

'I hope you'll keep my secret.'

'My lips are sealed.' Jake turned on his heel and hurried off to the kitchen. The woman had been right in the first place. He should've minded his own business and left her to her own devices. Tomorrow that was exactly what he'd do.

2

Jake ambled into the kitchen and froze at the sight of Hannah leaning against the counter. He'd hoped to beat her getting up and have his coffee infusion before facing her again. How anyone could look so serene and pulled together first thing in the morning was beyond him. He fought against staring, but her slim, dark jeans and a baby-blue T-shirt drew his eye along with her cool, appraising smile.

'You look bright-eyed and bushy-tailed. I guess you slept okay?' he mumbled.

'I slept very well, thank you.' Hannah set down the mug she was holding and grabbed another from the shelf, filled it from the coffee pot and held it out to him. Jake seized it with a grunt and sniffed at the strong, hot drink with relief. 'Not Mr. Sunshine, are we?'

He ignored her and yanked out a

chair and folded down into the seat, stretching out. Every morning when he got up with cramped legs and a stiff back, he missed his king-size bed.

'Is it all right with you if I leave my things here while I go and check things out next door?' Hannah asked.

'Yeah, no problem.' He glanced up at the clock on the wall. 'You'll want to call the utility people first thing to get on their list for reconnection.'

'If they can't do it today, I'll be finding other accommodation tonight.'

Jake almost smiled at her blunt statement but held back, guessing she'd string him up if he admitted her attitude reminded him of his bossy mother. 'Yes, ma'am.' Her eyes narrowed as though she suspected he was making fun of her. 'You want me to come with you?'

'Whatever for? It's an empty house. With you looming over the hedge ready to pounce on unsuspecting visitors, I'm pretty sure no one's dared to sneak in since my aunt died.' Hannah softened the barbed comment with a brief smile, although Jake wasn't sure she'd intended to.

'I was being a good neighbour, nothing more, nothing less.'

An instant flush of heat coloured her neck. 'I'm sorry. I didn't mean — '

'Forget it. I'm snappy this morning.' *Time to pull out affable, easygoing Jake again*. 'You go ahead, and if you need anything, let me know.'

'Thanks. What time do you leave for work?'

'Varies. I don't have a routine. I do gardening and odd jobs for people, nothing set. I'm not due anywhere until ten today.' Jake met her blatant curiosity without flinching. She was itching to question him more, but didn't dare. *Good*.

'I'll make sure I've got my things out of your way by then,' Hannah informed him, and turned around to rinse out her coffee mug before standing it on the draining board to dry. She faced him again, clearing her throat. 'I really do appreciate all your help.'

He nodded, and she started to walk

towards the door before suddenly stopping. 'Will you talk to me about Aunt Betsy some other time?'

Jake caught a thread of guilt and embarrassment running through her question. 'Sure.' He'd formed an unflattering opinion of Hannah's family from the conversations he'd had with Betsy and didn't look forward to the discussion.

'Thanks. I'll see you later,' she said lightly, and hurried out of the room, disappearing out the front door before he could be dumb enough to speak again.

* * *

Hannah gazed up at the washed-out blue sky with relief and was glad not to be plagued by any more storms of either the weather or man variety. She breathed in several deep, steadying lungfuls of fresh, salt-laced air and calmed down. Hopefully, away from Jake Walton's disturbing presence she could get her brain in some sort of normal working order.

14

She followed Jake's path around towards her aunt's cottage and mentally reviewed her plan to get the place ready to sell. Once she'd got rid of it, she could live on the proceeds while she planned what to do next. Working in the City again wasn't an option, thanks to Carlton Fenway. Hannah was considered the banking equivalent of Typhoid Mary because of her association with the man who'd fleeced millions out of his unlucky investors before fleeing to parts unknown. Apart from her family, nobody cared that she'd lost her own house and every penny she had in the process. The handsome Viking next door could flash his smile elsewhere, because she'd fallen for her last-ever charming man.

Hannah pushed open the gate and picked her way up the path over the broken flagstones and weeds that would need to be dealt with. Unfortunately, in broad daylight the house didn't look any more appealing. It plainly hadn't had a coat of paint in years, and when she ran her fingers over one of the windowsills rotten wood broke off in her hand.

Don't be feeble. She wielded the key and put it in the lock, turning it before she could change her mind. Then she flung open the door and marched inside. The stale air hit her straight away and forced her to leave the door open behind her. She stood still and looked around. The small, square living room certainly wouldn't win any prizes in an interior decorating competition. She guessed the dirty, water-stained walls were once cream-coloured, and the dull brown patterned carpet was beyond cleaning and needed to be ripped out and thrown away. Her gaze fixed on the sagging floral sofa in the middle of the room. On one end sat a pile of folded-up sheets, a worn grey blanket, and two pillows.

'Did you sleep here because you couldn't manage the stairs after you got sick?' Her voice echoed in the empty room and tears pressed at her eyes. No matter what had happened, they shouldn't have left Aunt Betsy alone and struggling.

Hannah tried to focus on the job at hand. She walked across the room and poked her head into a surprisingly large kitchen. The cabinets and appliances were woefully outdated and would take a lot to make appealing. A few steps further down the narrow hall, she stopped to open a door on her right. It was a cramped guest toilet, and by the small hand basin was a toothbrush, tube of toothpaste, and flannel. She guessed it was where her aunt had washed every day when she couldn't make it up to the bathroom. Hannah carried on and peered inside a gloomy dining room where the heavy dark furniture was all either valuable antiques or just old and ugly. From what she'd seen so far, she might have to *pay* any potential buyers to take the house off her hands.

Walking up a couple of stairs, she carefully picked her way around raggedy holes in the cheap brown carpet until she reached the landing. She instinctively opened the door on the left and was hit by the scent of violets.

'*Come here my 'andsome, and give your aunty a kiss.*'

'*Do I have to, Mum?*' she'd asked her mother the first time they came to visit, and could still picture the hurt on her aunt's loving face. After that, she got to know and love Betsy, looking forward to coming every summer. The year Hannah turned ten, their trips to Cornwall stopped, and when she asked why her mother said it was grown-up business. Later on she asked again, but was only ever told that Aunt Betsy behaved badly and the family wanted nothing more to do with her.

Drawn further into the room by her memories, Hannah walked over to stand by the dressing table. She picked up an antique silver-backed hairbrush and fingered the grey curly hairs stuck between the bristles. Aunt Betsy used to brush Hannah's hair before bed, always counting a full hundred strokes and never being in a rush. She picked up a round cardboard box decorated with yellow and white flowers, and before she even opened the lid she knew it would contain her aunt's favourite sweet-smelling pink face powder. As a treat, Betsy would dust some on her cheeks and then dab violet-scented perfume from a tiny cut-glass bottle behind Hannah's ears.

Gently she set the box back down. This wasn't getting her anywhere. Her first priorities were to get the electricity and water turned back on and then see about getting the roof fixed. After that, she would need to find someone to work on the windows and doors. No estate agent would touch the place until the basics were done. She could do the cleaning inside and sort through her aunt's things. Maybe if she was lucky it might be done in a month.

She slowly made her way back down the stairs, refusing to entertain the notion of falling and twisting her ankle or something equally stupid that would force her to call on Superman next door for help again. He'd already seen her being all girly over an idiotic storm, and she wasn't about to give him any more ammunition.

With one last glance around, she left and made sure she locked the door behind her. Back on Jake's doorstep, she prepared to knock, then realized the door was cracked open. Jake's voice drifted out: 'She's here already. I tried to warn you. Now what are we goin' to do?'

Hannah held her breath and waited.

3

Jake's brain registered a dead silence in the conversation. 'Yeah, I'm still here. Look, I want out of this.' His stepfather launched into a virulent tirade and didn't draw breath for several minutes before ending with a suggestion that made him laugh out loud. 'Charm her? You've got to be kiddin' me. She's an Ice Queen.' A sudden loud knock on the door took him by surprise but gave him an easy way out. 'Look, someone's here. I've gotta go. We'll talk later.'

'I'm back,' Hannah announced as she strolled in and sank into the nearest chair. 'I can see it's going to need some work.'

'Understatement of the year, sweetheart.' Jake plastered on a smile. He hadn't picked up on the click of the door opening, which left the possibility hanging that she might have overheard his end of the conversation.

'Could I hire you to clear up the garden?' Hannah asked. 'I need to tidy it up enough to sell as quickly as possible.'

He scrutinized her calm expression and decided she was either a very good actress or he was being paranoid. 'Sure, I'd be happy to help. I offered last year to do it for free, but your aunt refused.' It was the strangest conversation he'd ever had with his mild-mannered neighbour, because she had yelled at him and threatened to tell the police if he dared to touch a single weed.

'Thanks. I need to get a quote for the roof repairs and for having the window frames and doors worked on. Do you know anyone local who's any good?'

This was safer territory. It would please Christiansson to hear Jake was helping to get Hannah out of there. He told her about the Rashleigh brothers, who could turn their hands to anything. 'If you like, I could stop by and have a word with them on my way to work.'

Hannah's small smile made Jake feel he'd hit the jackpot. 'That would be great. And I need to call the electricity and water people. Once I've sorted that out, I'm heading into the village for cleaning supplies and to stock up on some food.'

'How about we meet at the Green Dragon for lunch and I'll give you an update.' *Why did you make that offer? You do not need to be around this woman any more than necessary.* 'Around one?'

'I suppose there's no harm in that.'

By her reluctance, anyone would think he was suggesting a great deal more than a simple pasty and a drink. Someone must have hurt her big-time. The sooner he got out of here, the better, before he made any other dumb suggestions. He'd spend the morning digging up Mrs. Truscott's vegetable garden ready for planting, and after lunch he'd get busy with his real job.

'Okay. I'd better be going,' Jake said. 'The key's in the door if you wouldn't mind locking up. Stick it under the red flowerpot outside on your way out. You'll find the phone book in the drawer over there.' He pointed at the small table by the window. 'The utility companies are listed in the front.'

'Thanks.'

He swept his wallet, phone and keys into his pocket and hurried outside.

★ ★ ★

Hannah watched Jake's retreating back, telling herself it wasn't to admire the tempting view. She would prefer not to notice he was a good-looking man. What she really wanted was to find out about the conversation she'd overheard. Recently she'd got pretty good at finding out things, even if the answers weren't what she'd hoped to discover. For now, she'd concentrate on working through her to-do list and reconsider Jake later.

Half an hour later, she gave herself a mental pat on the back. Hannah had spoken to a friendly lady at the water company and discovered the water at the cottage had been turned off after her aunt's death because the overdue balance hadn't been paid. She'd been able to settle up over the phone, paid the additional fee to get the water turned back on again, and was promised someone would be at the house around three that afternoon to get it sorted. Going through the same thing with the electricity company, she arranged for them to come in the afternoon too. By tonight she should be able to move in.

Hannah scribbled out a quick shopping list and then glanced in the mirror before deciding to brush her hair before she left. She ferreted around in her bag, then remembered she'd left her hairbrush in the bedroom. Hurrying back upstairs, she retrieved it before her nosey streak kicked in. Against her better judgement, she couldn't resist opening the door opposite hers to check out Jake's room.

She stepped inside and let out a long, low whistle. Downstairs was very ordinary, with its cheap furniture and bland décor; but this neat, masculine space clearly reflected the real Jake. The plain white walls with their framed nautical prints made a perfect background for the clean lines of his Scandinavian teak furniture. The top-quality dark navy bedding and curtains set it all off to perfection. Hannah walked over to the low, sleek dresser running along the far wall and checked out the couple of silver-framed photos. Obviously taken years earlier, they showed a teenaged Jake and a couple who, by their resemblance, must be his parents. One photo had been taken outside a large, imposing house, and the other showed them all gathered around a picnic table with a lake in the background. She shifted her attention to the bookcase, and the contents confirmed her suspicions that there was more to Jake than an affable, good-looking charmer. She knew it was pigeonholing, but was pretty sure not many odd-job gardeners read high-level economics and Aristotle in the original Greek.

'You're a mystery man, aren't you?' she spoke into the empty room, as though expecting it to tell her about its latest occupant. Then she leaned over to see what was on his bedside table. A well-thumbed copy of *Pillars of the Earth*, the Ken Follett tome she'd abandoned last summer, was on top of a Churchill biography and a thick computer programming book. Post-it notes with writing on stuck out of all the books, but she didn't dare examine them more closely in case she messed something up. Judging by how tidy the room was, she was pretty sure Jake would notice anything out of place.

Hannah walked out and carefully reclosed the door behind her before going back downstairs. Following Jake's instructions, she locked up and placed the front door key under the flowerpot. The supermarket in town would be cheaper and have more selection, but it wouldn't serve her purpose anywhere near as well. Village shops were renowned as an excellent source of gossip, and she'd love to find out more about her aunt and Mister Jake Walton.

The earlier chill in the air had faded, making it quite mild for early October. Walking into Polzennor would be a good antidote to the hours she'd spent in the car yesterday, but with all she had to carry back up the steep hill it was wiser to take the car.

Hannah started up her BMW, the last remaining relic of her previous life, and set off down the narrow, winding road to the harbour. Because it was late in the season, she found a parking space in front of one of the ice-cream shops and then wandered over by the wall to stare out at today's flat grey sea.

Brooding wasn't her style. She tended to be a practical person who got on with things, but it was hard not to allow regret to sneak in sometimes. Last year she'd become so wrapped up in her work that she hadn't seen the obvious where Carlton was concerned, and paid a hard price. Here in Aunt Betsy's house, she had discovered something else she should've paid more attention to, and wished she hadn't given up asking her mother what had caused the split with her only sister.

Hannah mentally told herself off. She was being stupid and wasting time. Before she could get any more introspective, she strode along the street and stopped in front of a small shop. The bell tinkled as she opened the door, and a grey-haired woman over by the counter stopped rearranging packets of cornflakes and turned to stare at her.

'My goodness, it's little Hannah.' Her shrewd eyes widened behind the thick glasses. 'You haven't changed a bit, my 'andsome.'

Hannah bit her tongue. If she *hadn't* changed from a plump, plain child, then the years spent improving her appearance had been in vain.

'Come here, my dear, so I can see you better.' The woman beckoned her over, and Hannah wended her between narrow aisles of shelves crammed full of everything the inhabitants of Polzennor presumably needed.

'Have we met before?' Hannah ventured.

'I'm Annie Rowse.' The older lady's friendly face creased into deeper smile lines. 'When you were a little thing, you used to come here most days shopping with your aunty. Betsy would ask what you fancied for your dinner and always let you have what you wanted.'

'Oh my goodness, I'd forgotten. But it's coming back now.' Hannah smiled with the memory. 'She spoiled me.'

'In a good way, my love. I'm some pleased to hear you've moved into Rose Cottage.'

'I'm only here temporarily to get it ready to sell,' she explained, and Mrs. Rowse's face fell.

'Oh, I were hoping you'd make it your home.'

Despite her mother being born here, Hannah was a London girl born and

30

bred, and wasn't about to vegetate in the wilds of Cornwall. 'I don't think so.' She must be careful not to be too rude or wouldn't find out the information she was after. 'Did you see much of my aunt before she passed away?'

Mrs. Rowse shook her head. 'Not really, my love. I used to pop up every now and then to have a cup of tea with her, but she weren't well enough to come down here for ages. She mostly got that there Jake from next door to do a bit of shopping for her.'

Perfect. 'Mr. Walton was very helpful last night when I arrived. He let me stay at his house because the power and water were off in the cottage.'

'I bet he did,' Annie chuckled, 'pretty girl like you. Better watch out or he'll have you in his harem.'

'Harem?'

'Being a gardener isn't the only reason he's known as Jake the Rake around here, my dear, if you get my meaning. The man flirts as easy as breathing. Mind you, he's a handsome one, and it wouldn't be no hardship,' Mrs. Rowse joked, and a touch of colour lit up her cheeks. Plainly few women, old or young, were immune to the man's charm. 'He's a good soul, though. Jake helped your aunty a lot, and I know several others he's done jobs for and not charged a penny. People think well of him around here.'

Hannah managed a tight smile. 'Has he lived here long?'

'About a year or so. They do say he's something to do with the man with the funny name, Christian something or other, who lives up at Polkirt House, but I don't know if that's right.' Plainly not knowing everything about everyone in the village didn't sit well with Mrs. Rowse.

'I'd better pick up the few things I came for.'

'Come down and have a bit of tea with me one day,' Mrs. Rowse offered.

'I'd like that, thank you.' Hannah got a brief flash of guilt for only agreeing because she wanted to pump the woman for more information. Luckily another customer came in, and Annie Rowse quickly turned away, no doubt to ask the new arrival for any fresh gossip. Hannah hurried around the shop selecting enough food to keep her going for a few days, plus cleaning supplies to tackle the accumulated dust and dirt back at the cottage. The surly teenager at the till took her money and haphazardly packed her bags before returning to playing games on her phone.

Back outside the shop, Hannah walked over to the car and stowed her bags in the boot. It was time to join Jake at the pub and find out a little more about the Greek-reading Romeo. She refused to ask herself why she was so interested.

4

Jake scraped his muddy boots on the cobblestones outside the Green Dragon and headed for the door, remembering just in time to lower his head before stepping inside. Fifteenth-century pubs weren't designed with oversized Scandinavians in mind, but he preferred this pub to the flashier Ring O' Bells with its slot machines and noisy teenaged crowd. *You're getting old, mate.* As he headed towards the bar, he checked around the room, but didn't spot Danger Woman.

'What're you having, Jake?' Roscoe asked with a friendly nod. 'Pint of Tribute?'

He hesitated. He had work to do this afternoon, but his usual soda-water and lime didn't appeal. 'Yeah, why not.'

'Pasty?'

'Better hang on. I'm expecting a . . . friend.'

'Another of your groupies? Don't know how you do it, mate. What's your secret?' Roscoe teased.

Jake could've replied that he wasn't overweight or balding, and had all his own teeth, but the middle-aged barman was a good friend of his. There was a lot about this place he'd miss when it was time to move on again.

'Bet your lunch partner just walked in.' Roscoe nodded towards the door and Jake turned to meet Hannah's cool green eyes. By the hint of colour tinting her cheekbones, she knew they were talking about her. 'Lucky sod.' His friend gave a sly grin and started to pull Jake's pint.

'Have you got us a table?' Hannah asked with obvious impatience as she reached him.

'Nope. Why don't you pick one and I'll bring a menu over. What'll you have to drink?'

'Orange juice, please. And don't bother with a menu — a pasty will be fine. I'm short of time.'

Jake would bet anything she was someone powerful in her other life. Hannah had the polite, borderline-abrupt manner of a woman used to being listened to and obeyed without question. He didn't care to analyze why it irked him. He'd always been a sucker for women with brains, but was getting a little too used to the ladies around here falling over themselves when he looked at them. Believing in his own carefully crafted reputation was foolish, which was not something Jake considered himself to be.

'Sure, I'll join you in a minute,' he said.

'I can hardly wait.' She mitigated the sharp words with a smile so brief he must have imagined it. There was no danger of his ego getting over-inflated around Hannah Green.

He watched her walk away, and a low whistle nearby made him remember where he was. 'Where'd you find this one?' Roscoe almost drooled. 'I haven't seen her around here before.'

'Temporary new neighbour. She's Mrs. Trudgeon's niece from London.' He dispensed the least information he could get away with. 'Not my type. Too full of herself.'

Roscoe stared as if Jake was mad. 'Need your head testing, you do. Take these and I'll bring the pasties over in a minute.' Roscoe shoved the drinks at him and shook his head in dismay.

Jake smiled but didn't make any comment, and headed over to where Hannah sat in the window seat overlooking the street outside. He chose not to slide in next to her on the narrow seat and instead pulled out the chair closest to him. 'There you go.' He set the drinks down. 'How was your morning?' He wasn't sure how to interpret the look she gave him, but suspected there was more to it than the surface revealed, which was next to nothing.

'Very productive, thank you. They're coming to turn the power and water back on this afternoon. I went into Mrs. Rowse's shop for a few things and we had a very interesting chat.' A teasing smile pulled at her pretty lips, hinting at things unsaid. 'She mentioned how kind you'd been to my aunt, Jake — or should I call you Jake the Rake?'

He forced out a broad smile. 'Call me what you like, sweetheart. Flirting hasn't been made illegal yet, as far as I know.' He was on safer ground now.

Hannah failed to stifle the rush of heat colouring her cheeks.

'Is something bothering you, honey?' Jake leaned in closer and rested his large hands on the table. She caught a hint of clean soap and guessed he must have stopped to wash before coming to eat, although it didn't mask the earthy aroma surrounding him.

'Should there be?' she retorted. 'Good grief, do you try it on with every woman between the ages of eighteen and forty?'

'There are age limits?' He laughed and flashed a white, toothy grin.

'Presumably even you have some standards?' *Priggish*. Carlton called her that when she turned on him over his creative banking methods.

'Don't *presume* anything where I'm concerned, sugar.' His deep, dark voice shivered through her and she caught a hint of his Danish accent beneath the American drawl. It made her wonder how much of Jake Walton's image was put on for effect.

'Two pasties. You want any sauces?'

Hannah stared at the plate and then up at the barman, meeting his curious stare head on. 'Not for me.' His face drooped and she guessed he'd been hoping for more in the way of conversation.

'Roscoe, this is Miss Hannah Green. She's Mrs. Trudgeon's niece and living up in Rose Cottage,' Jake cut in, his challenging tone no doubt done on purpose to show up her less-than-affable manners.

'Pleasure, miss.'

She made the effort to be polite and asked Roscoe about himself. It led to several minutes of conversation about the barman's family and what a good friend Jake was.

'I know you're busy.' Roscoe gave Jake a man-to-man grin, annoying Hannah in the process. 'But I want to pick your brains a minute. I told you my house sale was all but agreed, but yesterday someone called my estate agent and offered several thousand more. They didn't even bother coming to see the place. Seems odd to me, and you're sharp, so I want your opinion.'

Jake cleared his throat and looked embarrassed at the effusive praise. 'Would it mean you could buy the place you've got your eye on in Gorran?' The other man nodded. 'Can't see what the problem is. I'd seize the offer while it's out there. Doesn't make any difference to you who buys the house if their money is good.'

'Suppose not.' Roscoe shrugged. 'Thanks.' He went off and left them alone to eat.

'Are you happy now, Mr. Advice Guru?' Hannah couldn't resist teasing.

'Yeah, you could say that,' Jake replied, and gave her a self-satisfied grin.

Hannah picked up her knife and fork,

deciding the sooner she got this lunch over with the better.

'Forgotten the proper way to eat a pasty, have you?' Jake's rumbling laugh as he picked his up in his hands made the couple seated at the next table turn around and stare. 'Even a foreigner like me knows better.'

He was right, but if she did as he suggested, he would score another point on whatever score card they seemed to be keeping. Hannah continued to cut into hers and ignored his wicked chuckle. She ploughed on, not really noticing how it tasted because of the latent irritation pulling at her.

'I've got a couple of jobs on this afternoon, so if you're needing anything I won't be around much before six,' he said in his usual unperturbed way.

Hannah glanced up to meet his guileless blue eyes fixed on her. 'I can't imagine there'd be anything.' She left the words 'I'd need from you' unspoken, but she noticed his jaw tighten and knew he'd heard them. *Good*. 'I need to get on; I've a lot to do. Thank you for lunch.'

'You're welcome. Anytime,' Jake said with a sly nod. He swallowed the last of his beer and stood up. Hannah noticed he had to lean slightly forward to avoid hitting his head on the low rafters. He grabbed her coat from the seat and held it out for her to put on.

Without making a scene, she had no choice but to turn around and obediently slip her arms inside. Hannah was only too aware of Jake's warmth seeping through his worn plaid shirt as he stood a shade too close. As he smoothed her collar into place, she fought against pulling away from his unwanted touch. *Unwanted? Liar.* He rested his broad hands on her shoulders and leaned down to whisper in her ear, 'Remember, I'm only next door.'

'How could I forget?'

'Indeed.'

Jake stepped even closer, and Hannah's heart raced as he slid his other hand down her back to rest in the hollow at the base of her spine. Her throat closed and she couldn't make a sound. She didn't want to be kissed. *Really?* Then the anger that was never far away these days slammed back with a vengeance and she came to her senses. She shoved at Jake's chest and he took a step backwards, still giving her the same annoying smile. She hurried away and ran out of the door, followed by loud laughter. No doubt she'd be the talk of the place now.

Let them talk. She'd be gone soon and never come back.

5

'Women. Never can make up their minds,' Jake laughed over at Roscoe, and sat back down to finish his lunch. He refused to give the local gossips any more ammunition by going after Hannah. He'd embarrassed her enough. What the heck had he been thinking?

He pushed away the remains of his pint and stood up. It was time to see what Christiansson had for him to do today.

'Hey, Jake, are you coming back for the quiz tonight? We made a good team last time.'

He turned to face Pansy Winter's bright smile and forced down a groan. The blonde, bouncy surf shop owner was fun company, and normally he'd be up for the offer, but not today. She stood on tiptoe and draped her arms around his neck, fluttering her eyelashes at him, and he caught a glimpse of Roscoe's envious smile over her shoulder. 'Not sure yet, sweetheart.'

'Don't be a spoilsport,' she retorted, pouting her glossy red lips.

'I might make it, but don't wait on me.'

'You say that to all the girls,' Pansy complained. Jake resisted agreeing with her because it wasn't what she wanted to hear. She jerked her hands back down, placing them on her curvy hips and glaring so hard he was surprised she didn't go cross-eyed. 'Fine. Go and dig potatoes and I'll find someone else more reliable.'

Wouldn't be difficult. 'Sorry, love. I'll buy you a drink next time I'm in.'

'Don't exert yourself,' she snapped with a toss of her long blonde ponytail, and stalked off.

'Not your day, is it, mate?' Roscoe chided.

'You win some, you lose some,' Jake said easily. 'Plenty more fish in the sea.'

Roscoe polished a glass and held it up to check for smears. 'You'll be reduced to eating scraps soon, like the rest of us.'

'Yeah, well, I'll survive. Some of us have work to do. See ya around.' He left before his friend could bombard him with any more words of wisdom.

★　★　★

'Janik, have you finished playing gardener for the day?' Mikkel's booming voice rang out the second Jake stepped into the house. 'Get changed and come to my office. I've got something to run by you.'

Jake didn't bother to reply, but sauntered up the wide staircase, heading for the suite of rooms set aside for him to use. He closed the door behind him and slowly exhaled, then shucked his clothes and let them drop on the expensive Persian carpet before hurrying into the bathroom for a brisk shower. After drying off, he selected a clean blue shirt and pressed khakis from the wardrobe and got dressed. He smoothed down his unruly hair and prepared to join his stepfather.

It was time to put the first part of the day behind him and focus on his real work. They were close to completing the plans for a sprawling new resort based around this house. He hoped it would change the face of the local area for the better, bringing jobs and much-needed revenue to the village, although he wasn't sure the locals would agree.

Jake had spent the last ten months quietly acquiring property, under so many different names that their chief rival hadn't been able to pin down what was going on yet. The last piece of the puzzle was Rose Cottage; but when he'd sounded out Betsy Trudgeon about selling a few months ago, she'd told him where to go in no uncertain terms. Now there would be a further delay. His hope of completing a swift sale long-distance with the new owner safely tucked up in London wasn't going to happen. Instead he was stuck with beautiful, sharp-tongued, interfering Hannah. There was no way she'd be content to sell to an anonymous buyer, and if she discovered his involvement that would be it. Something Betsy told him once about Hannah was nagging at him, but couldn't get it to connect in his brain.

Mikkel would send one of his minions to track Jake down if he didn't hurry up. Reluctantly, he headed off to listen to his stepfather's newest bright idea. The property development business used to fascinate him, but these days he got more pleasure out of planting cabbages and turnips. That wasn't a fact he planned to share with anyone.

★ ★ ★

Hannah brushed away a strand of loose hair from her face and glanced around the room with a satisfied smile. She wouldn't be able to start cleaning until the utility people came, so had made the most of the daylight to start sorting through her aunt's bedroom. She'd already filled up ten large plastic bags, earmarking some for the charity shop and the rest to be put out with the rubbish. Out of nowhere, a piercing stab of sadness ran through her and she dropped down on the bed, digging her fingernails into her palms to stop from crying.

The paltriness of it all had got to her — this reduction of someone's life to a stack of black bags. She hadn't found anything she wanted to keep, which in itself was sad. Would someone feel the same one day sorting through her own belongings? Hannah supposed her designer clothes and expensive make-up would be sent to Oxfam or the nearest dump. She was usually happy to leave the past where it was and concentrate on moving forward, but since her neat little world had fallen apart she'd had far too many dark moments.

The sensible thing would be to pay someone to clear the house; put it in the care of an estate agent to get on with selling it while she carried on with her life. *Life, what life?* At almost thirty, she wasn't about to move back into her childhood home. But she was almost out of money, and with no job prospects the alternatives weren't exactly piling up.

'Miss Green, are you there? It's Andy from the water company. I did knock.' A deep male voice drifted up the stairs and brought her back to earth in an instant.

'Yep, I'm just coming.' Hannah stood up and brushed off her dusty jeans. Closing the door behind her, she made her way slowly down the stairs herself to avoid the treacherous carpet.

'Andy Wareham. I'm here to . . . ' The man's warm brown eyes crinkled at the edges and a shy smile lit up his face. 'I don't believe it, it's little Hannah all grown up,' he said with a shake of his head, and glanced down at the form in his hand. 'It never occurred to me 'Ms. H. Green' could be you.'

She gave him a swift, appraising glance — about her age, average height, and pleasant-looking in a normal sort of way. Nothing registered.

'Don't know why I'd think you'd remember me.' He gave a self-deprecating laugh and ruffled a hand through his thick black hair. 'You stayed here with your aunt several summers, a long time ago. I lived a couple doors down, and Mrs. Trudgeon would get my mum to send me over to play.' A tinge of colour sharpened his cheekbones. 'I'm afraid to say I used to call you Hannah Banana.'

'Oh, my goodness, it's you!' Hannah squealed. 'Your horrible toy army men kidnapped my favourite doll and tore off her head. When I cried and ran in to Aunt Betsy, you laughed at me.'

'Sorry! Am I forgiven?' He gave her a shamefaced smile.

'I suppose so,' she laughed. 'Do you still live here?'

'No. My mother does, but not for much longer. She sold up the other day and is moving in with my aunty in Truro. I've got my own house over in Mevagissey.'

No doubt along with several kids and a wife too — decent men like him always did. It wasn't that Hannah had some burning desire to settle down, but she did wonder sometimes.

'On my own,' he replied with a hint of quiet disappointment.

For a moment Hannah didn't know how to respond. If she said she was in the same situation, it would sound a touch desperate, but if she didn't answer at all it would seem unfriendly.

'Me too. Fancy free.' She hoped she gave the impression she was fine with her solitary state. Mostly she was, especially right now when getting involved with another man would be akin to swallowing a cyanide pill.

For a second their eyes met, and he gave a sympathetic nod. A film of tears blurred Hannah's vision and she stared down at her feet.

'I'd better get your water turned on. I've still got a couple more stops to make before it's knocking-off time. I'll do it outside at the street and then come in to make sure everything's good.'

Hannah wanted to hug him for changing the subject. 'Of course. Thanks. I'll let you get on with it and be in the kitchen if you need me.'

She planned to make a start on sorting through the cupboards, but instead went to stand by the window and stared out over the back garden. When Andy came back into the room, she stood to one side as he fiddled around under the sink and ran the taps for a few minutes.

'You should be all set.' Andy straightened back up. 'I'll be off.' He hesitated a second. 'I don't suppose you'd like to have a drink sometime . . . I mean, just as friends; I'm not — '

'I'd enjoy that,' she said, surprised to find she meant it. 'I'm not here for long, but it'd be good to catch up. How about sometime this weekend?'

'Friday?'

'Fine.'

'Will the Green Dragon down in the village be okay?'

Bumping into Jake while she was out with Andy wouldn't be conducive to a pleasant evening. 'How about somewhere

53

in Mevagissey instead? I'd love to go there again.'

They made their plans and Andy went on his way, leaving Hannah to wonder why she'd said yes to his offer. Then the doorbell rang, and she sighed with relief. She'd been saved from any more introspection by the electricity board.

6

Jake popped open the cold beer can and took a long, welcome swallow. Back in his comfortable old clothes again, he'd gravitated to the small patio at the back of the house and stretched out on the wood recliner he'd made himself over the long winter nights, as he savoured the cool evening air. Women always complained about his ingrained Danish habit of having his house windows open year round. He'd grown up wearing as few layers as possible, and it still had to be freezing cold before he'd put on a coat.

He glanced across the hedge and noticed Hannah's lights were still on. The possibility of going over to apologize came and went. He could go to bed, but the frequent middle-of-the-night shifts he worked to conduct business with the US, combined with far too much time-zone-crossing travel, had screwed with his sleep schedule.

As he replayed his conversation with Mikkel in his head, it didn't get any better. They needed to wrap up buying Rose Cottage within the month, because rumours were beginning to swirl around, and it wouldn't be long before they would be forced to make things public. He'd agreed to try hurrying Hannah along by being a good neighbour and offering to help her get the house ready to sell. Short of making a straight-out offer to buy, there weren't any other options — not any legal ones he was willing to consider, anyway.

Jake drained the can dry and crushed it in one hand. The slight tired buzz lingering around his brain allowed in the possibility of wandering over to his neighbour to agree a time for him to work on her garden. *Liar. You're aching to see her again. Nothing to do with cutting her damn grass.* He unfurled his legs and stood up for a good stretch. He'd deal with the consequences later.

Hannah knew she should be exhausted. It was past ten o'clock and she hadn't stopped all day, but her body buzzed with suppressed energy. Every time she stopped for a second, Jake's quirky smile filled her vision, and she wondered what she would have done if he *had* kissed her. Why she'd even chosen to sit outside in the overgrown, freezing-cold garden was a question she couldn't answer.

She must be going crazy. For a second she could've sworn she smelled a hint of Jake's clean scent in the crisp night air.

'Hey, neighbour, enjoying the warm weather?'

Hannah glanced up. She hadn't been imagining things. 'What are you doing here?'

Jake stood perfectly still with his attention fixed on her, his ice-blue eyes glinting in the moonlight, and her insides churned into knots again. 'Thought I'd make sure you got all fixed up today and didn't need the comfort of my home again.' A slow, lazy grin eased across his handsome face. 'Plus, I wanted to see if it was okay for me to work on your garden tomorrow. I'm free until mid-afternoon.'

'What happens then? Do you turn back into Cinderella when the clock strikes three?' Teasing was her best defence against the attraction she didn't want to feel for this, or any, man.

'I work for Mr. Christiansson at Polkirt House later in the day.'

'Doing what?'

He raised one eyebrow. 'What do you think? I'm a gardener.'

'Of course you are. How could I forget?' Hannah left the words hanging, and a sudden flush of colour darkened the sharp slash of his cheekbones. 'That's fine with me. I've got plenty to do indoors.' She was trying to think of the best way to get rid of him, without actually wanting to. 'I was about to make some coffee, if you'd like some.'

'Are you sure?'

'I wouldn't have offered if I wasn't,' Hannah retorted.

'You could be doing the polite English thing. Even after living here off and on for years, I'm not great at working out if y'all mean something or not. It's gotten me in trouble a few times,' he said with a shrug.

'I can believe that.' He was rattling her again. 'Oh, for goodness sake — if you're staying, sit down and be done with it. I'm only offering you coffee, not anything else.' Her attempt at teasing made her skin burn with embarrassment.

'Pity,' he drawled. 'I'll take you up on the offer anyway.' He glanced around. 'There seems to be a chair shortage. Want me to bring my own over?'

'I'll fetch one out from the kitchen. Take mine.' Hannah jumped up and hurried indoors, sensing his eyes following her all the way.

Hannah Green, you're an idiot. She concentrated on getting their coffee ready and placed the two mugs on a tray along with a plate of chocolate digestives. At the back door she hesitated for a moment and watched Jake. He'd made himself comfortable with his long legs stretched out in front of him and his large hands clasped behind his head.

'I'm not gonna bite, honey, so come on out.' Jake turned his head and beckoned her over. When she didn't move, he stood up and strolled over, closing the gap between them with a couple of large loping strides. 'I'll get the other chair.'

She cleared her throat and tried to speak, but gave up and simply nodded.

Jake stood to one side and as he let her walk by his arm brushed hers, disconcerting her with his touch. Hannah hurried away and set the tray down on the unsteady wicker table she'd dug out earlier from in the shed. She quickly sat back down into the deckchair.

'Here we go.' He reappeared and settled the upright kitchen chair next to her on the grass before sitting down. Hannah picked up the other mug and held it out to him. 'Thanks.' Without another word he blew gently on the coffee and started to drink. 'Heck, that's good stuff, Hannah. You must have brought this with you. They don't sell anything this decent at Rowse's and your aunt, bless her heart, was a definite tea person.' Jake tossed her a mischievous grin. 'Unlike her heretic of a niece.'

'What did she say about me?' The question tumbled out before she could help herself.

Jake scrutinized her hard and took another long swallow of coffee before speaking. 'She missed you. Betsy wasn't a woman to share her family business with strangers, so don't you go thinkin' that. She told me there'd been some sort of family argument and y'all weren't speaking.'

Hannah set her mug down and rested her hands in her lap to hide the fact they were shaking. 'I wish she had told you more. My mother won't say either.'

Putting his coffee back on the table he leaned over and took hold of her hands, wrapping them around with his own warm, strong fingers. 'Maybe they had good reasons.'

'I don't care,' she protested, 'I need to know. Poor Aunt Betsy died here alone and struggling. That wasn't right.' She yanked her right hand out of his grasp to brush away a tear rolling down her face. Before she could try to stop them, more tears followed. Next thing she was sobbing uncontrollably — something she hadn't done in years, even when Carlton ruined her life.

Jake dropped down on his knees in front of her and pulled her into his arms. Hannah rested in his comforting warmth and cried into his soft hair.

'She wasn't alone, honey. She had plenty of friends in the village and they all visited and took care of her.'

'You're just saying that to make me feel better,' Hannah argued.

'Nah, that's not my style, I'm not good at the whole sugar-coating thing.

It's the truth. I know the house was a wreck, but that's because she refused to let anyone tidy up or clean. She was a stubborn woman, very proud,' Jake said with a grin, 'like someone else I know related to her.'

Hannah pretended to smack him and almost lost her balance in the process.

'Hey, be careful, or we'll both be on the ground. Not that I'd object, but it might be hard on the back muscles.'

'You're awful.' She managed a luke-warm laugh.

'Like it though, don't you?'

'I refuse to answer on the grounds it might incriminate me,' she teased right back — something she thought she'd forgotten how to do. Carlton didn't have much of a sense of humour in the first place, and there hadn't been much to laugh about recently.

Jake eased back and cradled her face with his hands, stroking his large thumbs up and down her cheeks. 'Better now?' He stared right into her and Hannah forgot how to breathe. Everything else went away and all she saw were his extraordinary ice-blue eyes fixed on her. His tempting mouth was so close she caught the aroma of coffee on his breath. 'This isn't right, Hannah.' Regret ran through his voice.

'Why?' she whispered. 'Don't you want to kiss me?'

He slid his hands down to rest on her shoulders. 'Oh, Hannah, of course I do, honey. But . . . there are too many reasons why it's a bad idea.'

'Would it be such a hardship? I'm not asking for anything more.'

Jake's laugh rumbled through her. 'You really think either of us would be satisfied with that for long?'

'But we only met yesterday.'

'So?'

Hannah came to her senses and she remembered she was talking to. This was a man who'd no doubt flirted with every attractive woman within a twenty-mile radius, at the very least. 'How could I forget? Your reputation precedes you. How stupid of me.'

His face hardened, and for a second she wished she could take back the words. 'You know nothing about me, and nor do the people here.'

'Tell me then. I dare you,' Hannah tossed out the challenge.

Jake shook his head, took hold of her hands again, and eased them both up to standing. 'Thanks for the coffee. I'll be over in the morning.'

'That's it?' she pleaded, and his face softened.

'All I'll say is, don't believe every-thing you hear. People often do the math wrong when they add two and two together, don't they? You of all people should understand.'

A shiver ran through her blood. 'What exactly do you mean?'

'Come on, sweetheart. I may be a gardener, but I'm not dumb. It came to me earlier about something your aunt said once. All it takes is Google these days. Carlton Fenway. Holborn Broth-ers. You know all there is to know about being falsely accused.'

'Get out,' she hissed, on the verge of tears again, 'and don't come back. I'll get someone else to do the garden.'

'But, I . . .'

Hannah ran away and stumbled into the kitchen before slamming the door shut behind her. She would have slapped him across the face if she'd stayed and had never done that to anyone in her life. What she couldn't bear was that he'd told the truth.

7

The combined scents of lavender air freshener, pine disinfectant, and lemon furniture polish irritated Hannah's throat, so she threw open the windows to the fresh air. Two solid days of scrubbing and polishing had left the house gleaming. At least now any potential buyer should make it further than the front door. Next on her to-do list must be the neglected garden. How difficult could it be to pull up a few weeds and cut the grass? It would have to wait until at least Monday, because there was rain in the forecast for the weekend. Instead she'd concentrate on the boxes of her aunt's papers and photos she'd put to one side while she cleaned.

She had time to do a quick shop in the village before having lunch and cleaning herself up for going out with

Andy tonight. Hannah checked her appearance in the mirror and cringed. She couldn't even go to buy a loaf of bread looking this awful. She shook out her hair and re-brushed it before ruthlessly pulling it back in a tight ponytail, then swapped her dirty work clothes for a clean black long-sleeved T-shirt and fitted grey trousers. The whole effect was funereal, so she added a swipe of scarlet lip gloss — though a mental picture of Jake's lazy smile as he almost kissed her made her grab a tissue and wipe her mouth clean.

The brisk walk down to the village helped, and by the time Hannah reached the harbour she'd calmed down. She stood and watched a couple of dog walkers on the beach and a lone surfer before heading towards the small post office. After she bought a few stamps, she headed next door to the shop and hoped against hope that Mrs. Rowse wouldn't be working. But the moment she stepped inside, the idea of a quick escape evaporated.

'Hello, my dear. I haven't seen you for a few days. You might want to pick up a packet of Hobnobs if they're not on your list.'

The woman's conspiratorial smile puzzled Hannah. 'I've got biscuits already, thank you.'

'Not Andy Wareham's favourites, you don't, I bet,' she said with a decided smirk, and a rush of embarrassed heat flared up Hannah's neck.

'We're only having a drink together,' Hannah protested. 'He's an old childhood friend, that's all.'

Mrs. Rowse immediately launched into a long, detailed explanation of Andy's qualities and managed to make him sound like a cross between Colin Firth and Gandhi. If he was so perfect, why hadn't he been snatched up before now? Hannah chided herself for being mean.

'I'll go ahead and pick up what I need, thank you.' She forced herself to be polite, which was quite a challenge when she wanted to tell the nosey old woman to mind her own business. She'd had enough of people interfering with her life and passing judgement.

Luckily the same morose teenager was on the till today, and the would-be Goth with her black lipstick and pierced eyebrows didn't care who Hannah was or wasn't going out with. No doubt she considered anyone over the age of twenty-five as dried up and of no interest.

Hannah picked up her two Hobnob-deficient bags and made her escape. Outside the door she hesitated. Why shouldn't she go into the Green Dragon for a pasty if she wanted to? Enough stubbornness trickled through her blood to give her the courage to walk towards the pub.

She stepped inside and gazed around the room, looking for any oversized Danes. The few other customers acknowledged her existence but didn't make any effort at conversation, which suited her fine. She was relieved to see Roscoe wasn't behind the bar, and made quick work of ordering before taking her pear cider over to the empty window seat.

Last time she'd only got a quick impression of old wood beams, dark well-worn furniture, and a slate floor pitted with age. Now she studied the whitewashed walls more closely and noticed the scattering of black-and-white photos of the village and the harbour as it had once been years ago, a vibrant port full of small fishing boats. Her gaze rested on one of a group of fishermen sat on a bench, smoking their pipes and obviously talking about the state of the world. Some of them could be related to her, and for the first time she felt a glimmer of interest beyond getting out of here as soon as possible.

'They could tell a few stories, couldn't they?'

As she glanced up, her mouth went dry.

'Mind if I join you? Or am I still an outcast?' Jake teased. 'I'll risk taking your silence as a yes.' He set his glass down on the table and pulled out a chair. Hannah didn't speak as he drank half his soda water down in one long swallow before taking a break. He fixed his attention back on her and she couldn't look away, no matter how hard she tried.

'I'm sorry.'

'What for?' She wasn't about to make it easy for him.

'Being an idiot the other night. Don't know what got into me. Seems I forget all my manners around you.' He shrugged, and Hannah wanted not to notice the bunched-up muscles shifting temptingly under his old grey T-shirt. What was wrong with her? Anyone would think she'd never seen a good-looking man before.

'Nothing to be sorry for.' She needed to be honest, because the opposite had got her in too much trouble. 'You were perfectly right in what you said. I was being too sensitive.'

Jake gave her a penetrating stare. 'It's tough when things become public that you'd rather not have the whole world see. I know.' The rasp in his voice hinted at emotions she was sure he would rather stayed hidden. He was offering her a window into the real Jake Walton, but she knew it wouldn't take much for him to close the curtains again. For now it was enough to ease the tension between them. She gave a tentative smile, and the tautness in his broad shoulders eased.

'How about I make a start on your garden tomorrow, and we go from there?'

Hannah guessed weeds were as good a place to start as anything.

'Unless you've found someone else to do the job?' he asked and she shook her head.

'I was going to tackle it myself,' she ventured and Jake grinned. 'Is it that amusing?'

'Nah, wouldn't dare to say that, sweetheart. I value my life too much.'

She basked in the glow of Jake's relaxed smile for a few moments.

'There you go, two pasties.'

Matching plates were slammed down

in front of them and before Hannah could thank the young waitress, she tossed her mane of jet-black hair over her shoulder and flounced off.

'What was that about?' Hannah asked, and Jake stared down at his food.

'That's Maddie. We've been out a couple of times, and — '

'Ah, she's another of your harem? I should've guessed.'

Jake gave a long, heavy sigh. 'Hey, I'm a single man who enjoys the company of women. I never make promises I can't keep.'

'I'm guessing that to be on the safe side, you rarely make any at all,' Hannah jibed, and he winced.

'Pretty much.'

She'd bet anything there was a lot more to it. 'Fair enough. I know where I stand now.'

'I didn't say it applied to you,' he growled. Hannah stamped down a smile and guessed he hated making that concession.

'How about we eat our pasties and

leave it at that for a while?' Before he could answer, she picked up hers and took a large bite. 'Oh, boy, that's so good. I didn't appreciate it last time, but I do today.' She caught a hint of humour in his eyes. 'And yes, I remember how to eat it the right way now, too.'

'Good girl.' Jake's impish grin widened. Then he picked up his own to start eating, and for the first time in ages Hannah relaxed. She was determined to make the most of the moment instead of worrying what would come next.

When they were both done, Jake moved his chair back and stretched out, resting his hands behind his head in his favourite position. 'I've been craving a decent hamburger all week, so I'm firing up my grill tonight. You wanna join me?'

Hannah hated to refuse, but had no choice. As she explained where she was going, his expression changed, the smile replaced by an unreadable blankness.

'Maybe some other time then. I've got work to do. Better get going,' he announced, and stood up. 'If it's not raining, I'll be over in the morning.'

'Thanks,' she replied to his retreating back as he walked away. She smiled to herself and reached for her coat to get ready to leave, but something lying on Jake's chair caught her eye. On the seat was a slim black case that must have fallen out of his back pocket. Hannah turned it over in her hands and admired the top-quality leather. She flipped it open to check it did belong to him and saw a stack of business cards. Without thinking, she slid out the top one and read the details. She didn't know why she was in the least surprised.

Janik Eriksen. International Property Development. There was an email address and mobile phone number too. Hannah's mind whirled around in circles. *What international property developer sets up as an odd-job gardener in Cornwall,* she wondered, *and pretends to be nothing more than a good-looking flirt who's handy with a rake?*

A knot of disappointment settled in

the pit of her stomach. She'd survived years of working in the City with a lot of ethically dubious people — some would say she'd been one herself — but she hadn't pinned Jake as being that way. From day one, the gardener story clearly wasn't all there was to say about him, but in her tin-pot way Hannah had imagined him as maybe a burned-out teacher needing a break.

Idiot. You've the character judgement of a slug. With a heavy heart, Hannah slipped the case into her handbag and wondered whether or not to return it to Jake. Did she want him to know she knew? But how could she face him again and say nothing? The heartbreaking moment when she realized what Carlton had done slammed back, and she bit her lip to stop from crying. She'd paid the price for her hesitation the day the police turned up on her doorstep.

When Jake came to tackle her garden, he'd have a lot of explaining to do.

8

Jake's stomach growled, and he checked the time in the corner of his computer screen, surprised to see it was ten o'clock already. Too late to cook any hamburgers tonight, but no one was waiting for him, so it didn't matter. The work day was winding down on the east coast, but he still needed to get in touch with his colleagues in San Francisco before they finished for the weekend. Once he wrapped up this project, he planned to head across the pond to start on acquisitions for another of the Christiansson company's boutique spa resorts.

He rubbed at the headache pulling at his temples and allowed Hannah back into his awareness, even though it was a bad idea. At lunchtime he'd been intrigued when the sun picked out reddish lights he'd never noticed before in her sleek blonde hair. It had stirred his imagination, making him wonder what it would look like loose around her shoulders. He couldn't afford to be tempted, but he was. Sorely.

'Wrapping up soon, son?'

Jake glanced back over his shoulder and managed a tight smile. His own father had died when Jake was fifteen, but it didn't give Mikkel the right to call him 'son'. 'I'm about to call Paul Harding, then I'll be done.'

'Any big plans for the weekend?'

Jake shrugged. 'Not really.'

'Your mother's coming down from town tomorrow and it would make her happy if you join us for lunch on Sunday.' Jake knew the invitation was only being made for her sake. 'Bring a friend if you like.'

'I can hardly do that, can I?' Jake snapped. They both knew it was essential to keep up the carefully constructed distance between them where business was concerned.

'You made your mother a promise.'

'Yeah, and I'm keeping it, but not for

much longer. You'll have had your payback soon.'

'I'm the one who'll decide that.' Mikkel's cold words hinted at the real man behind the facade of an urbane Danish business-man. 'Elsa wasn't the one who kept you out of prison.'

'You know I didn't do anything wrong,' Jake protested, gripping the arms of the chair.

'Do I?' Mikkel's voice lowered. 'One o'clock Sunday. No excuses.'

'Yes, sir.' Mikkel would pick up on the irony lacing his words, but neither of them would openly acknowledge the fact. He turned back to focus on his computer, and didn't relax again until his stepfather left the room and he was alone.

★ ★ ★

Hannah's eyes ran over the abandoned clothes strewn all over the bed. Everything was too something — too date-worthy, too dressy, or too obviously London.

Did Andy consider this a real date? If he did, how did she herself feel about the idea? After her discovery about Mister Jake Walton, or whatever he was calling himself today, her emotions were in a muddled-up mix. Over-thinking was one of her biggest faults, but the last time she let her guard down with Carlton she'd ended up bankrupt, unemployed, and only escaping prosecution by the skin of her teeth. From now on she'd think about every decision until her brain exploded with the effort.

It's a drink and perhaps a plate of fish and chips. Don't be silly. Hannah selected the black trousers and turquoise silk blouse nearest to her and quickly pulled them on. Before she could change her mind, she added simple gold hoop earrings and slid a trio of gold bracelets onto her right wrist. She sat down at the dressing table, and for a second her hand lingered over her aunt's box of face powder that she hadn't had the heart to throw out yet. Pushing it to one side, she opened her make-up bag and added a touch of mascara and a slick of pink lipstick to brighten up her pale features.

Hannah made it downstairs just as the doorbell rang. 'Aren't you looking pretty?' Andy said, and his appreciative smile warmed her.

'You clean up well, too.' Hannah was glad she'd smartened up when she saw his own well-pressed navy slacks and crisp white shirt.

'I can't have you thinking we're all yokels down here,' he teased. 'Come on, let's go and paint Mevagissey red.' Andy slid her hand in through the crook of his elbow in a pleasantly old-fashioned way and they walked together down the path. 'I even cleaned my car out, so you're honoured.'

Hannah checked out the smart late-model black Volvo with a touch of surprise. *You're judging people too quickly again. Stop it.* 'I am indeed,' she said lightly as he opened the door for her to get in.

She'd forgotten what it was like to simply enjoy someone's company with no ulterior agenda. They never stopped talking on the drive there, while they walked around the pretty harbour, or the whole time they were eating dinner. Once Hannah even laughed out loud, and couldn't recall when that last happened. There was no frisson of attraction either, at least not on her side, and that made it easier.

'So, are you ready to indulge in a pudding?' Andy asked.

'No, thanks. I'm full. The scampi was delicious, but I shouldn't have eaten enough chips to feed a whole family,' she joked. 'We could go back to my place for coffee if you like.' But she instantly regretted asking. 'At least, I — '

'It's okay, don't panic, I'm not expecting anything.' As he emphasized the last word, she managed a smile. 'Don't get me wrong, you're a lovely woman, but I'm not interested in you that way either.'

'Oh.' Hannah couldn't decide whether or not to be offended. She wasn't Miss World, but being turned down so bluntly was disconcerting.

A gentle smile lit up his face. 'It's not you, it's me. I asked you out because I could do with a friend, and sensed maybe you could too.'

Hannah wondered if he knew about the troubles she'd had, deciding he must do, seeing as how they'd been plastered all over the newspapers. She nodded and squeezed his hand. 'Thanks.'

'You're welcome.' He gave her a piercing stare and sucked in a deep breath. 'Let's just say my wife wouldn't be happy if I made a move on you.'

Hannah's jaw dropped and she couldn't think how to reply as a million and one questions raced around her head.

'It's complicated. We have our reasons for not being together right now and keeping things quiet. No one in Polzennor knows.' There was a warning tone to his voice.

'I won't say a thing. Don't worry,' she hurried to reassure him. 'Mrs. Rowse would be struck dumb. She tried to force a packet of Hobnobs on me to seduce you with.'

84

'I'm not *that* easy,' he joked. 'It takes at least two packets.'

They laughed together, and Hannah couldn't help but wonder at the different direction the evening had taken, and how much better it was now that things were straight between them. 'You'll have to make do with pink wafers I'm afraid,' she said. 'I had a childish longing for them when I was in the shop.'

'They're my second-favourite biscuits, but we'll keep that from Mrs. Rowse too,' Andy whispered, and gave her a wicked grin.

Hannah stifled a giggle. 'You're impossible. Take me home so I can pick your brains about Aunt Betsy.'

'I'd be delighted.'

They left the pub and headed back to Polzennor. As Andy stopped his car outside Rose Cottage, Hannah's gaze strayed next door, despite her intention not to look. There weren't any lights on, so presumably Jake was out chatting up more girls. The idea needled her far more than it should have.

'I hear your neighbour's quite the local Romeo.' Andy's warm laughter brought her attention back.

'I wouldn't know. I've barely met him.' Hannah tried to appear indifferent. 'I suppose he's good-looking if the obvious blond Scandinavian type appeals to you.' *Cut my heart out with a blunt knife for being such an appalling liar.*

His eyes sparkled. 'The lady doth protest too much, methinks.'

'Goodness, a man who quotes Shakespeare correctly.'

'I don't spend all my time connecting water pipes,' Andy declared.

A hot blush flooded Hannah's face. 'Sorry. I didn't mean to imply — '

'You're very easy to tease, you know that?'

Before she could answer back, Jake's battered old truck drove up behind them, sending the loose gravel flying as he turned into his driveway. Hannah couldn't see anyone else in the car with him.

'Come on, Hannah, lead me to the pink wafers.'

She wouldn't spend any more time considering where Jake had been or with whom. 'Let's go.'

They got out of the car and she linked her arm with Andy's, telling herself it was necessary to negotiate the dark, uneven path and nothing to do with the fact that Jake might be watching.

9

Jake wandered outside to the patio and stretched out on the recliner, shoved a cushion behind his head and kicked off his shoes. As he glanced across the garden, the lights went on in Hannah's kitchen. No doubt her date was being treated to some of her excellent coffee. Jake had seen them wrapped around each other as they walked in a couple of minutes ago. He popped open a can of beer and drained it in a couple of swallows before opening a second one, then gave in to the tiredness creeping through his body and allowed his eyes to close.

He startled awake as the can dropped from his hand and beer dripped all the way down his arm, soaking the sleeve of his shirt. 'Damn.' Today wasn't his day. He pulled off the wet shirt and tossed it onto the grass. The air was chilly, but he couldn't be bothered to move anytime soon.

Voices drifted across from next door, then a car door slammed and an engine started up.

'Don't you ever feel the cold?' Hannah's smiling face appeared over the top of the privet hedge.

'Nah, we Danes have ice for blood.'

She gave a fake shiver. 'How unpleasant.'

'Fancy a beer?' He wasn't sure how to read the expression on her face. It was as though he'd asked a deeper question than whether she was in the mood for lager.

'Not really. How about you come over for coffee instead?'

'Didn't your boyfriend finish it all?' Even in the dim light Jake saw her eyes darken.

'Checking up on me, are you?'

He saw no need to lie. 'I saw you arrive and heard him leave.'

'So what? Have I asked who you've been out with tonight?' Hannah snapped.

'No, because it's none of my business.'

'Hey, I didn't mean any harm,' Jake hurried to placate her. 'I'm sorry. Anyway, I haven't seen any women all evening.' He carried on before she could ask too many questions he couldn't answer. 'Is your offer still open?'

'I suppose so.' A faint smile tugged at her lips. 'Put a shirt on before you come.'

'Afraid I'll distract you?' he joked, and was rewarded by a charming blush lighting up her face. 'Will do. I'll be there in a minute.'

★ ★ ★

Why couldn't she stay away from the stupid man? Hannah asked herself. She should have gone on up to bed instead of hanging over the hedge like a desperate teenager with an unrequited crush. She forced herself to concentrate and got a tray laid ready to take into the other room when Jake arrived.

'All right to come on in?' He stood over by the open back door and waited until she nodded before stepping inside.

The room appeared to shrink as he came to stand in front of her, and she found herself inches away from his broad chest, now covered in a respectable blue shirt. Instantly she was aware of his warm, clean scent and glanced up to meet his intense stare.

'I really want to kiss you,' Jake murmured, his Danish accent thickening and making her heart race. 'But I don't want to tread on anyone's toes.'

She realized he was talking about Andy and managed not to laugh. 'Andy's a good friend, that's all.'

'Are you sure?'

'Definitely.' A satisfied smile crept across Jake's face. 'So, am I ever going to get that kiss?'

'You sure are.' He slid one hand down around her waist and pulled her closer while his other hand reached around and tugged at the tortoiseshell clip holding her hair in place. He tossed it down on the counter and shoved his fingers through her hair, shaking it loose around her shoulders. 'Beautiful.'

Finally. His warm, firm mouth found hers and she sighed, giving in to his wonderful kiss. A low growl escaped the back of his throat and Jake eased away with a heavy sigh.

'Heck, Hannah.' A slight tremble ran through his voice.

'Maybe we should drink that coffee now.' Hannah stumbled over her words.

'Coffee?' Jake's hoarse laugh resonated around the room.

'One of us needs to have some common sense. After all, you haven't even shared your real name with me yet.' It was the last thing she'd intended to say, but desperately needed some protection against the surge of emotions running through her.

Jake's hands dropped back down to his sides. 'What do you mean?' The dark, quiet words disturbed her more than if he'd yelled.

Hannah forced herself to walk over to where her handbag hung on the back of one of the kitchen chairs. She searched in the outside pockets and found what she was looking for. Turning back around, she held out the small leather case, and Jake took hold of it between two outstretched fingers as if it was a poisonous snake.

'Where did you get this?'

'I think it dropped from your trouser pocket when we were having lunch yesterday. I found it in the chair after you left and opened it to make sure it was yours so I could return it. If not, I would have handed it in at the bar.'

Jake rested his massive hands on her shoulders and the heat from his spread fingers burned through to her skin. 'I owe you an explanation.'

'You don't owe me anything.'

He leaned down to press a soft kiss on her mouth. 'Yes, I do.'

'How about we sit down and have coffee.'

'No more kissing?' His tentative smile, so unlike his usual cocky manner, drew her to him more than ever.

'Better not,' she said kindly. 'Go into

the other room and I'll bring our drinks in.' She needed to get herself under control before she listened to what he had to say.

Jake dropped down onto the sofa and stretched out his legs. *Look relaxed.* She didn't need to know how knotted up he was inside.

'Help yourself.' Hannah placed a colourful round tray on the low table in front of him and pointed at one of the steaming mugs.

He picked it up and inhaled the fragrant brew before taking a sip. 'Ask what you like.' *I'm not saying I'll answer, but . . .*

Hannah looked sceptical. She probably had as much faith in him telling the truth as in the idea of Miley Cyrus going into a convent. *Wise woman.* 'Go with the name first.'

'Janik's my Danish name. I use Jake around here because it's easier and doesn't draw attention to my background.'

'Why would that matter?'

She wasn't going to make this easy,

but why should she? For the first time ever, he wanted to tell a woman everything, but couldn't for a multitude of reasons. 'Let me explain about my real job.' The tightness around the edges of Hannah's mouth told him she was bothered about what he might admit. From what he'd seen online, he'd got a handle on some of what she had gone through recently, and it wasn't pretty. 'I work in property development.'

'Really. That's a surprise.' Hannah's caustic manner made him wince. 'I guess that's why it says that on your business card. You're not telling me much, are you?'

Her cool sea-green eyes pinned him down, and it was all he could do to sit still. 'I travel around the world buying up land for a client who's into developments of different kinds. There are times when it's better not to be too obvious about what I'm doing until the job's finished.' He watched the wheels click and turn in her head. It wasn't hard to predict the next phrase out of her mouth.

'So what are you doing here?'

Mikkel would skin him alive if he blabbed. Jake set his mug down and rested his hands on his knees. 'I honestly can't say. There's a clause in my contract that bans me from discussing the plans with anyone.' Hannah nodded, and he let out the breath he hadn't been aware of even holding.

'Fair enough,' she said.

'Really?' Jake couldn't believe she was letting him off this easy.

A shadow crossed her pretty face. 'For now. I won't be here long, and you won't either is my educated guess.'

Jake didn't deny it and suspected he'd been put on warning. He picked up Hannah's hands from her lap and cradled them in his own. 'Can kissing go back on the agenda now?'

A teasing smile crept across her face. 'It certainly can, but remember what I said.'

'Oh, I will,' he replied as he swooped down to indulge them in another wonderful kiss. He would push the issue away for tonight and worry again in the morning.

10

Hannah sat the first cardboard box down in front of her on the kitchen table but made no move to rip it open. Although a slight drizzle clouded the windows, it didn't stop her from making out the shape of Jake moving around in the garden. He'd appeared on the dot of eight that morning with a bag full of fresh chocolate croissants from the village bakery, and they'd enjoyed a leisurely breakfast together. She was relieved when he'd asked no questions of her in return for the snippets of information he'd shared with her last night. She didn't plan to mention him to her mother anytime soon, not after Janie had turned into a fierce, protective lioness over the whole mess with Carlton.

All this wasn't getting Hannah anywhere so she picked up the scissors and slit through the wide brown tape. She opened back the top and lifted out several albums, hating it when the unpleasant musty smell rising up from the mildew-spotted leather made her sneeze. Last night over dinner Andy had shared a few bits of information he'd pried from his mother, but they didn't help to sort out what had caused the family split. Apparently Aunt Betsy had become very withdrawn about the time Hannah stopped visiting and started to neglect herself and the house. When her neighbours complained about the state of the garden, she'd got angry, which fitted in with Jake's description of Betsy's reaction to his offer of help.

Hannah pushed the box to one side and sorted out the albums in front of her by putting them in date order. She started to flip through the older ones and smiled at photos of her mother and Betsy as children back in the early 1970s, and later as teenagers with their arms around each other. They'd been inseparable . . . so what had stopped them speaking to each other for nearly twenty years?

Hannah put the album to one side and opened up the next one. The first photos were of her parents' wedding in 1984, her mother wearing a short white dress and flowers in her hair, laughing up at her handsome father.

'Any chance of a cold drink for a hard-working bloke?'

Hot tears pricked at Hannah's eyes, and she jerked her head up to meet Jake's smiling face.

'Hey, what'd I say? I'll get it myself, don't fret.' He leaned against the open door and started to kick off his muddy boots.

She shoved her chair back out of the way and jumped up. 'No, stay where you are. It's not you . . . it's all this.' She gestured towards the albums, and the words dried in her throat. Before she could make it as far as the sink, Jake caught up with her and pulled her into his arms, wrapping her around with his warmth.

'Bringing up memories isn't all it's cracked up to be sometimes, is it?' he murmured against her hair. 'You want to show them to me?'

'What about the garden?' She struggled not to be a wimpy, emotional woman.

'The rain's comin' down pretty heavy now, honey. I was goin' to quit anyway.'

She became aware of how damp his soft red flannel shirt was against her cheek and sucked in a deep breath. It wasn't easy to admit she wanted to take him up on his offer, but managed a brief nod. 'Okay. You sit down. I'll fetch a drink and we'll look at the photos together.'

For some reason, she didn't mind him telling her what to do, and soon they were sitting side by side at the table. Jake draped one arm around Hannah's shoulder as she picked up the next album. She saw the date, 1994, written on the spine and swallowed hard. Then she opened up the first page and blinked back another rush of tears. 'That's my ninth birthday party, at our home in Watford. It's the last time I remember seeing Aunt Betsy.' She touched her fingers to the picture of her own round smiling face as she stood in front of a garish pink Barbie birthday cake ready to blow out the candles. She spotted her father hovering in the background, his face pale and serious. 'That's my dad. He left us the next day.'

'I'm sorry. Are you still in contact with him?'

She shook her head. 'He died the following year, in a fight outside a London nightclub.'

'I understand. My father died when I was fifteen.' The sadness threaded through his words. Tears dripped unbidden down Hannah's face and she was helpless to stop them. Jake pulled a clean white handkerchief from his jeans pocket to gently wipe her cheeks.

'He used to call me Princess. He said I was the smartest and most beautiful girl in the whole world.'

'You are,' Jake said with such certainty that it drew her to meet his unwavering gaze. Before she could say something unwise, she forced herself to turn away.

Hannah's hands shook as she continued to rifle through the box. All she found were a random selection of later photos, mainly of village events, but no more family ones. She tossed them aside and slammed the box shut. 'I need to know.' She surprised herself with the fervour of her words. 'It's important.'

'Is there anything else that might give you any clues?'

She pointed to a couple of smaller boxes on the floor. 'I skimmed through those the other night. They seemed to mostly be letters and financial records, but maybe they'll have something important in them.'

Jake leaned in to touch her chin, tilting it towards him. 'Why don't we have a bite of lunch now and then settle down to go through them?' He hesitated for a second. 'I don't mean to butt in. If you'd rather look at them in private, say so.'

'I'd prefer to do it together.' She couldn't resist giving him a quick kiss. 'Why don't you go and wash up while I make us some sandwiches? You need to get that wet shirt off.' Her cheeks flamed as he broke into a wide grin. 'I mean, put on something dry instead.'

'And where would you like me to get a spare one without going back to my house in the rain and getting even wetter?'

'Smart, aren't you?' Hannah teased. 'I found a couple of large men's shirts in the back of Aunt Betsy's wardrobe. They're clean but paint-stained, so I'm guessing she wore them doing decorating to cover up her clothes. I expect she bought them at a jumble sale. I'll bring one down for you.'

'That'll work. I'll go and clean my hands.' Jake eased himself out of the chair and headed towards the downstairs toilet.

Maybe coming here to clear out the house hadn't been her worst idea ever, Hannah thought.

★ ★ ★

Jake took his time, scrubbing his nails and trying to drag a comb through his damp, unruly curls. The feelings he had for Hannah confused him. It wasn't just that he wanted to kiss her, and more, but he ached to wipe the sadness from her eyes. She'd been through so much and hated anyone to see what she considered to be her weakness. The last women he'd had a real relationship with was a pretty doctor called Karena he'd met in Copenhagen. She left him nearly two years ago because he wouldn't be open with her about his past. In Polzennor he'd gained a reputation as a ladies' man by being considered good-looking and liking women enough to actually talk to them.

'Are you coming to have lunch, or have you drowned in there?' Hannah's lilting voice called to him.

'Sorry to disappoint you. Still alive.' Jake half-opened the bathroom door and stuck out his hand. 'I'll try it on and see if it fits.' He peeked his head around and took the old grey work shirt from Hannah's hands. 'I'll be out in a minute.'

'Thanks,' she whispered, and a rush of heat lit up her face. The touch of vulnerability only enhanced her beauty, but Jake kept that to himself.

'What for?' he asked her.

'Being patient with me.'

He didn't know how to reply. 'No problem, sweetheart. You go see to lunch and I'll be with you in a minute.' The last thing he wanted was to hurt her, but he knew it was probably going to happen. He longed for things to be different, but his life seemed to work that way.

11

Hannah glanced at Jake, who was hunched over the table and toying with his ham sandwich. They'd made polite conversation for the last ten minutes with none of the previous ease they'd shared earlier.

'Are you still bothered about me finding out what you're doing here?' she probed. 'It doesn't matter to me if you're digging up people's weeds while you buy up property around here. You know I'm not planning on staying. I'm selling this place, and . . . ' A cold shiver of reality trickled down her spine. 'Is Rose Cottage on your acquisitions list?' Jake's silence was her answer. 'Did you need to go this far? For heaven's sake, I'm sure even *you* don't go around romancing every woman you do business with.' Her anger grew. 'Say something. You owe me,' she snapped.

Jake reached for her hand but she pulled it back into her lap, unable to be touched by him and think straight at the same time. 'Us . . . this . . . was never about business,' he said.

'But you do want to buy the cottage?' she persisted.

'Yeah, but I . . . ' He fixed her with his ice-blue eyes and she couldn't look away. 'You fascinated me from the first moment you slapped me down in that icy British way. I should've made a straightforward offer for the house, but my business demands a little more discretion. Anyway, you want to sell, don't you?' he asked, sounding puzzled.

'Yes,' she conceded. 'But it's not that simple. I will when I'm ready. What I don't get is why anyone wants this ugly house. It's not exactly a showpiece, is it?'

'I can't say,' Jake murmured, and she couldn't read any emotion in his stern features. 'I'm buying on behalf of someone who doesn't want his plans made public yet.'

Everything started to fall into place. 'Roscoe — that's you too, and Andy Wareham's mother. You have to know people are going to start asking questions.' He didn't confirm or deny her suspicions, only gave a resigned shrug. 'Your lame explanation doesn't wash with me. I've been messed about by one devious businessman. I understand about confidentiality, but I need to know I'm not being made a fool of again.'

'I wouldn't do that to anyone, and certainly not you.'

The quiet certainty in Jake's words almost convinced Hannah he was telling the truth; but a vivid picture of Carlton, his eyes full of tears and his hands shaking, slammed into her. He'd dragged a Bible from the bookshelf and placed his hand on the worn black leather before swearing he'd done nothing wrong; that he was being harassed by their bank's vice president. She'd foolishly believed him and signed over the last of her money, only to be left high and dry when he cleared out the account and fled the country.

'I'm not Carlton Fenway,' Jake whispered, his Danish accent thickening.

Hannah folded her hands in front of her. 'No, but you aren't Jake Walton either, are you? I think you'd better leave.' She wished more than anything that he'd fix his intense stare anywhere else but on her, but he never even blinked.

'Is that what you want?'

Asking him to be honest was one thing, but doing the same herself was another matter. She couldn't lie. 'It's what I need.'

Jake nodded and pushed the chair back to stand up. Hannah dug her fingers into her thighs, wishing she could stop herself from drinking in the sight of him. He was too muscular and work-hardened to be on the pretty side of masculine, but she'd had enough of men who took longer to get ready to go out than she did.

'I'm off,' he said. 'Unless you tell me otherwise, I'll still get your garden done. I never leave a job unfinished.'

Do I come under that category?

'You were never a job, honey. If there's anything you need, you know where I am.'

Only too well. Hannah sucked in a deep breath as he stepped towards the door, brushing past her as he went. Knowing she'd done the right thing didn't help the crack in her twice-broken heart.

★   ★   ★

Jake trudged down Hannah's sad excuse for a garden path and around to his own house, registering the fact it was still raining but past caring. He'd left his tools outside Rose Cottage but they'd have to stay there for now. His phone started to buzz and he retrieved it from his jeans pocket. There was a message from his stepfather demanding he come to Polkirt House tonight. Jake cursed under his breath and tapped in a quick reply to tell Mikkel where to go before turning off the phone.

The worst thing was that this wasn't only about Hannah. Before this, he'd never got close to people he was doing business with; but things here were different. In the last ten months he'd grown fond of the village and the people who'd taken him at face value. Even his reputation as a ladies' man was always accompanied by a smile. Roscoe was his friend and wouldn't understand the story behind the increased offer on his house. In theory Jake hadn't cheated him, but it didn't alter the fact that it had been done in secret and would result in Roscoe's treasured house being demolished.

Jake glanced back over at Hannah's back door, but it remained shut. The idea that she might run after him was beyond dumb, and she was one smart woman. *Too smart for you. Forget her.* He dragged off his muddy boots and left them to one side of the step. He'd fix a pot of coffee and sit down and think. Giving up on Hannah wasn't an option, even if for now that was what he'd have to let her believe.

A couple of hours later he'd drunk enough coffee to put him into a caffeine coma, and needed food. He dragged himself into the kitchen and took a hunk of Havarti cheese from the fridge, hacking off two thick slices before slapping them on top of some dark rye bread. Standing over by the window, he sank his teeth into the open sandwich and forced down several large bites. About halfway through he gave up and tossed the rest in the bin.

Someone started to pound on the front door and Jake groaned. Whoever it was, he didn't want to see them.

'Open up, Janik. I have no time for your nonsense.'

His stepfather kept on shouting. He wasn't a man to be ignored. Jake should have remembered that when he'd sent the dismissive text message.

'Hold on.' He strode out into the hall

and flung open the door. 'Draw attention to yourself, why don't you?' He glowered and hauled the other man in, slamming the door shut behind him. 'My gardening clients don't normally yell when I miss a spot of weeding. That's what you're supposed to be, remember?'

Mikkel ignored him. 'I tried to call again but your phone wasn't on. What did you expect me to do? There is a problem and it cannot wait until the morning. I do not do this for my own amusement, Janik, I thought I'd made that clear many years ago.'

Jake didn't bother to argue. There was no point. He gestured to his stepfather to go into the living room. 'Coffee?'

'I do not have time. We have guests arriving in one hour and your mother is already unhappy with me. That is a situation which does not please me.'

Jake suppressed a smile. The only person Mikkel Christiansson feared was the petite, quietly spoken Elsa, who didn't need to say anything but only give her errant husband a certain look and he gave in. 'Sit down and tell me what's up.' He dropped down into his favourite chair, rested one leg up on his knee and waited.

Mikkel paced around the room. 'Pedersen is sniffing around,' he announced. 'We need to wrap this up fast. The little lady next door must sell, and I don't care if you have to sweet-talk her.'

'Don't you dare talk about her that way,' Jake hissed. He glanced away, disgusted with himself.

Mikkel's unkind laughter filled the room. 'Did she turn you down? My sources tell me the women around here are throwing themselves at you. This one must have more taste than I gave her credit for. I do apologize.'

'Get out — now,' Jake growled.

'Not until I make my expectations clear. Tomorrow you will bring me a plan for finishing this job in one week. That is the longest I can keep things quiet. Pedersen is checking on properties in the

St. Ives area, and if he opens up a resort there it will destroy my plans.'

Jake knew he should keep his mouth shut, but it had never been one of his strong points. 'Why is he bent on destroying your business? Isn't there enough space for the two of you to have your fancy hotels and spas without treading on each other's toes?'

Mikkel's countenance hardened. 'Let us say it is something that runs deep. All I need is for you to do your job.' He turned and headed back into the hall. Jake did as he was expected to and followed. 'You will come at noon tomorrow and see me before lunch.'

It wasn't a question. Jake would have to turn into Houdini to escape from his stepfather's clutches.

12

Hannah studied the birthday party photograph for about the fiftieth time. Something niggled at her but she couldn't nail it down. She massaged her left temple and wished the throbbing headache would go away, like Jake. She'd spent ages going over their conversation before deciding to do something more constructive. Presumably that was why she was back in the kitchen, surrounded by her aunt's old albums again but still thinking about Jake. No matter how she looked at it, the conclusion was the same — that he'd fooled her for his own ends. The fact she had told him she intended to sell was nothing to do with it. But the deeper truth was that as each day went by, Rose Cottage changed in her mind from a rundown house she planned to sell to fund her new life, to something far more — something she couldn't, or wouldn't, put a name to yet.

Her finger on the photo lingered on her dad's pale, gaunt face. She'd been too wrapped up enjoying her party to notice how bad he'd looked, but no doubt the knowledge of what he intended to do the next day had been hanging over him. Hannah briefly considered ringing her mother, but the questions would be the same as every other time since she'd come here. How was she getting on? How much longer before she could get the cottage sold? When was she returning to London? The answers were not very well, no clue, and maybe never.

Never? The idea was ridiculous. She needed to get out of the house before she went completely crazy. Before she could change her mind, Hannah ran upstairs to the bedroom, pulled her hair back into a neat ponytail, and slicked on a layer of red lipstick. She didn't bother to change out of the black sweats and white jumper she'd put on after Jake's abrupt departure.

Hurrying back downstairs, she decided

to walk into Polzennor and blow away some of the cobwebs. She seized an umbrella on her way out of the door as a precaution, although the earlier rain had stopped, leaving a pleasant evening that could almost have hinted at summer if not for the fading daylight.

When she arrived down at the harbour, Hannah hesitated near the Green Dragon, then kept going all the way over to the Ring O' Bells. Loud, thumping music throbbed out through the half-open door, and the drift of raucous laughter stopped her from walking any closer.

'It's grim. Not your style. Don't bother.' Roscoe's soft voice by her ear startled Hannah and she jerked back around. 'I'm going in to work. Come along and prop up the bar for a while.'

'Maybe I prefer somewhere lively.'

His raised eyebrows were the only reply to her stupid comment.

'Fine, I suppose I could.' She'd have to take the chance that Jake wouldn't turn up too.

'You don't have to talk to anyone if

you don't want to.' A touch of sympathy lurked in Roscoe's warm brown eyes. 'I rang Jake earlier and he about bit my head off. Don't think he's in a sociable mood tonight.' He started to walk away and Hannah fell into step beside him, not replying straight away. 'It's none of my business, love; I won't be poking around.'

His plain speaking made her smile, and as they reached the front door of the pub she put her hand on his arm. 'Thanks.'

'No probs, love. We look out for our own here, and your aunty was one of us.' The blunt statement took her by surprise, and she could only manage a tight nod as Roscoe threw open the door and gestured for her to go inside. That was something else to think about when she couldn't sleep tonight.

★　　★　　★

The second glass of red wine softened the edges of Hannah's odd mood. A group of good-humoured middle-aged women were playing darts over by the fireplace; she guessed they'd escaped their families for a couple of hours and weren't in a hurry to return. Roscoe was getting in everyone's last orders and chatting with a couple of locals who'd been propping up the bar alongside her all evening.

'Some idiot offered more than the asking price, but I'm taking it before he changes his mind,' Roscoe said with a smile.

'From up London way, I s'pose?' one of the men asked, obviously curious.

'Dunno. Estate agent's a bit cagey, but don't matter to me so long as I get my money.'

'You'll care right enough when they tear it down,' Hannah blurted out.

'What're you talking about?' Roscoe's round, placid face hardened.

She'd better be careful. 'I might be wrong. Forget it.' She decided to leave before she made a fool of herself.

Roscoe reached across the bar and

placed a hand on her arm to stop her moving. 'Hang on. You can't say crazy stuff and then clear off. Where'd you get that idea from?'

The other customers were all openly listening by now. Why shouldn't they know they were being taken for fools, too? 'Your good friend, Jake,' Hannah stated flatly.

'What the heck has Jake got to do with anything?'

'Open your eyes,' she challenged as anger got the better of her common sense. 'The charming, womanizing gardener persona is nothing but a front. Jake isn't even his real name. It's Janik Eriksen. He's a highly educated half-Danish property developer, and he's been buying up houses and land around here for a client.'

The colour drained from Roscoe's florid face. 'You sure?'

'Yes. Well, about some, and I've guessed the rest from what he wouldn't say. If I were you, I'd tackle him and make him tell you the truth.' She picked up her glass and drained the rest of her wine in one swallow. 'I'm off, but I'll tell you one more thing — I won't be selling Rose Cottage to Jake Walton or whoever he's working for, and if he doesn't like it that's tough.' She stared defiantly around the room.

'You okay to walk home?' Roscoe asked, his voice slightly unsteady.

'Of course I am.' Half-sliding off the bar stool, Hannah walked over to the door and felt everyone watching her all the way out. She stumbled as the cold air hit her face. She stood still and sucked in a few deep breaths before starting off in the direction of her house.

Halfway up the hill, a wave of tiredness swept through her and she considered sitting down for a while to rest, but a few brain cells kicked in and told her not to be stupid. The sky was pitch black and heavy with threatening rain, while the wind had picked up and was whipping in off the sea. This wasn't the smartest idea she'd had recently, and she'd had a few dumb ones.

She plodded on, and as she rounded the corner the sound of heavy footsteps thumped towards her and a scream rose in her throat. She fumbled in her pocket for her phone, but it wasn't there. 'Damn.' A clear picture of placing the object in question on the bar came to mind and she groaned. Hard, cold raindrops started to spit against her face, and she pulled her coat in tighter. A loud roll of thunder rumbled through the sky and she couldn't hold back a panicked scream.

'It's okay. You're fine.' A huge dark shape loomed in front of her face and strong male arms wrapped around her. She lashed out, kicking wildly and coming into contact with an ankle and a knee before wriggling around enough to jerk her own knee up between the man's legs. Thank goodness she'd done one sensible thing this year and take a self-defence class.

'It's me, Jake. Did you have to do that?' He groaned and sank to his knees. Lightening crackled out over the sea, sending a jagged flash straight into the black waves, and Hannah let out another scream. Jake instantly jumped back up and wrapped his arms around her again. This time she buried her head in his thick warm coat and sobbed. Somewhere on the edges of her terror, she realized he was stroking her hair and murmuring soothing words into her ear.

'Let's get home before we're soaked again. This is getting to be a bad habit,' he joked.

'At least I'm perfectly capable of walking this time, so you won't have to do your caveman bit.'

'Good job one of us is capable. You've about finished me off.' He grunted and seized hold of her hand, tucking it into the crook of his elbow.

'Sorry,' she muttered.

'Yeah, well, it's my fault for not speaking up. You weren't to know. I'll recover.'

'What are you doing down here anyway? Bit late for a walk, isn't it?' She almost tripped over her feet trying to keep up with his long-legged stride.

He turned and gave her a fierce glare. 'Why do you think? Roscoe was worried and rang me up to come look out for you.'

'Oh.' She shut up and kept walking while things bumped around her confused brain. 'Did he, uh, say anything — '

'About your outburst in the pub? What do you think? Course he did. I'm gonna have a talk with him tomorrow. We were both more worried about you than anything else tonight.'

A rush of heat flamed up Hannah's neck, zooming towards her face at warp speed, and she was grateful for the cover of darkness. 'Thanks.'

He didn't reply, and for once she decided silence might be her smartest move too. They turned into Pilgrim's Road and walked past Mrs. Wareham's house, then Jake's, to arrive at Rose Cottage. At the door Hannah hesitated, unsure of the etiquette concerning thanking a rescuer if you'd kicked them earlier in the day.

'Forget it — it's late and best left for now,' Jake said quietly, and let go of her hand while she unlocked the door. 'You'll be okay?'

About the bad weather? The fact you fooled me? The yearning I've got for you to kiss me again? All of the above? Hannah slapped on the bright professional smile she'd made good use of the last year while her world fell apart. 'Of course.'

Jake inched closer and his warm breath brushed over her face, making her heart pound in her chest. 'Tomorrow evening. Supper at eight.'

'But — '

He pressed a soft kiss on her forehead. 'Give me a chance. Please.' Before she could answer he walked away, leaving her confused and irritated at how weak-willed she could be around this intriguing man.

13

Roscoe ignored the glass of whisky on the table in front of him and gaped open-mouthed at Jake. 'A spa resort? What's one of those when it's about?'

His stepfather would kill him when he found out he'd told his friend the truth, but Roscoe's bewildered curiosity dragged it out of him. He didn't want to lose another friend. *Another? He's the only one you've got.* Jake hated the fact that he'd left a trail of would-be friends and acquaintances in the trail of his work over the last few years.

Jake explained about the resort without going into too many details. 'It'll bring a number of new jobs to the area and encourage more tourists. That has to be good, right?'

'Tearing down perfectly good houses, building on decent farmland and bringing more Londoners to the village year-round instead of only in the summer. Wonderful, mate.' Roscoe's biting sarcasm sliced through Jake. 'You took us all for fools, didn't you?'

'That wasn't my intention.'

Roscoe's disgusted snort expressed his reaction as clearly as if he'd spelled it out the words. 'You told Hannah all this?'

Jake shook his head, and for the first time in an hour Roscoe smiled. Not his usual friendly smile, but a satisfied smirk that said they both knew what she'd do to him.

'It's time I got off to work.' Roscoe heaved himself up to standing and trudged over to the door. 'Good luck. You're going to need it when this gets out, pal.'

Jake didn't bother to reply. After the door slammed behind his friend, he picked up both their glasses and took them into the kitchen. If he didn't start walking over to Polkirt House now, he'd be late. Annoyed with himself and everything in his life, he sat back down and decided to make Mikkel wait for a change.

* * *

Thank goodness the overnight rain had stopped. Hannah decided to test her theory that hard work would stop her thinking about Jake. A few hours of scraping paint and sanding might help, but if it didn't at least she'd have made a start on the windows.

She took off her pyjamas and threw them on the bed before pulling an old pair of jeans out of the drawer. Then she opened the wardrobe and dug around in the back to find one of the men's shirts she'd discovered the other day. She slipped it on and buttoned it up. Glancing in the mirror, she froze. She fingered the worn blue check material and admonished herself not to be silly. Lots of men had similar shirts. It didn't mean anything.

Barefoot, she walked back downstairs and out into the kitchen. The albums were still strewn around the table as she'd left them. She picked up the last one she'd looked through while Jake was there. Every time, the same ninth birthday picture drew her back. She focused on her father and rested her finger on the shirt he was wearing, then glanced down at her aunt's old shirt and slowly exhaled. Crazy. She must be going crazy. Even presuming it was the same one, what did it mean? Anything? Nothing? Before she could overthink things, Hannah pulled her mobile out of her pocket and put her mother on speed dial.

'Hello, dear. I hope you're ringing to tell me you're coming home soon?'

'Do you remember my ninth birthday party?' she blurted out, unable to make polite conversation. Her mum's audible indrawn breath told her she'd been right — this was important. 'I found a picture in Aunt Betsy's album.' The silence filling the line was deafening. 'Do you want me to describe it to you?'

'That's hardly necessary. Why are you

being so cruel? You know very well what happened the next day.'

But Hannah couldn't let it go now. 'Do I? I know Dad left us, but you never explained anything else.'

'It was all you needed to know, and still is.'

Hannah changed the direction of her questions to see what might happen. 'Why did you fall out with Aunt Betsy?'

'It was between the two of us, and nothing to do with you,' Janie stated in the tone of voice she always used when she didn't intend to add any more to what she'd already said.

'But I loved her and missed her very much. From what I've heard, she apparently missed me too, so you're wrong.' She was tired of this only being about the two sisters.

'You wouldn't feel the same way if you knew what she did,' her mother snapped down the phone.

'Knew what? Tell me,' Hannah persisted, but only got a heavy silence in return. She'd toss out a wild card, she decided, and see what reaction that stirred up. 'This is off the wall, but something else is confusing me. The shirt Dad is wearing in the birthday party picture resembles one I found in Aunt Betsy's wardrobe. I wore it to do some painting and couldn't think why it seemed familiar, until I spent a long time looking at photos yesterday.'

'Oh, Hannah, why can you never leave things alone?' Janie gave a resigned sigh. 'You've always been such a contrary child.'

Hannah didn't bother to contradict her mother's accurate summary. It wasn't the first time she'd been called stubborn.

'This isn't something to discuss over the phone. I can't get away until next weekend, but I'll come down on Friday and we'll talk.' Exasperation ran through her mother's voice. Hannah suspected she should feel guilty for upsetting her, but giving in wasn't her style.

'Thanks.'

'You won't thank me by the time I'm

through, but it's your choice,' Janie said in a clipped tone, and hung up the phone without telling Hannah she loved her.

For a while Hannah stood there clutching the phone and fighting back tears. What she wouldn't give for some of Jake's compassion right now, and to have his strong arms wrapped around her again. She forced herself to remember he was still a liar and a conman. He was no better than Carlton.

She stripped off the blue shirt and replaced it with one of her own brown T-shirts. It was too good to work in, really, but she didn't care. Physically wearing herself out was the only way she'd get through the day.

Supper at eight.

The question was whether she would turn up. She'd given men enough chances before now, and look where it had left her: alone, jobless, and reviled in the financial community where she'd made a good living. If she could get her hands on Carlton Fenway, she'd give him a sample of the punishment she'd meted out to Jake when she thought he was about to attack her last night. At least one man wouldn't take her for a wimp again anytime soon.

She hummed to herself as she made her way out to the shed at the far end of the neglected garden. Jake had made a dent in the mess yesterday, but it would take a lot more work to even get it presentable. She opened back the door and checked out the supplies she'd bought. She'd selected a rich dark red paint for the window frames and front door, which should enhance the house's grim facade. The Rashleigh brothers were coming to start the roof repairs tomorrow, and afterwards they'd tackle most of the painting.

She started work and didn't stop for hours, until her cramped shoulders and aching back wouldn't let her keep going any longer. A surge of satisfaction ran through her as she stood back and admired the progress she'd made. The ground-floor window frames were all rubbed down and sanded, ready for priming. She'd prepared the front door as well, and in a flash of determination decided to paint it herself when everything else was done. It would be her statement of ownership, and she didn't care if Jake liked it or not.

Voices drifted over the hedge from next door. She could pick out Jake's deep voice, but the other belonged to a woman. *What a surprise.* Hannah crept over and crouched down in the overgrown flowerbed backing up to the high privet. The woman spoke in what Hannah guessed to be Danish. She might not understand the words, but scorn sounded the same in any language.

'I'm too tired to think in anything other than English today,' Jake objected.

'What a surprise. Look at you! You're a disgrace. Your father would be ashamed.'

'Oh, give me a break. You always invoke his memory when it suits you. The rest of the time we're not allowed to mention his name, and I'm supposed to put up with that man calling me 'son'. He makes me sick.'

Hannah barely managed to stop herself from toppling over in the mud as the clear sound of a face being slapped rang out, along with a string of what must be Danish swear words. This wasn't Jake's weekend.

'You will present yourself at the house at six. We both expect an apology for your tardiness — and I understand Mikkel has some business to discuss?'

'Yeah.' Jake's grouchiness was evident and Hannah smiled. He wasn't having much luck with women at the moment.

'Oh, Janik.' The woman's voice lowered and softened. 'You're a good boy. I know you have a lot to put up with.' Hannah pinched her nose to stifle a sneeze. 'Life is not always what we would hope, is it? I will leave now. Go and sleep.'

'Yes, *mør*.'

Hannah heard heels clicking along the path and waited for Jake's door to shut so she could move.

'You can come out of hiding now. I hope you heard everything,' Jake's

137

caustic voice boomed out, and Hannah tried to stand up but tripped over her feet and fell headfirst into the long grass. Wiping wet mud from her hands, she got up and turned around, face to face with Jake's fury. If they were in a cartoon, he'd have smoke coming from his ears, and if she was honest she couldn't blame him. Ice-blue didn't describe his eyes today, because there was no trace of colour in his steely glare.

'Sorry. I . . . uh . . . didn't mean to listen.' It sounded pathetic, even to her ears.

'You just *happened* to be kneeling by the hedge, I suppose?' Jake persisted. 'That was my mother, if you're interested.'

'So I guessed.' There was really no point pretending otherwise. 'She didn't sound happy with you.'

He rested his elbows on the privet hedge and Hannah couldn't avoid his searching gaze. 'She rarely does. If you're good, I might tell you all about her over supper.'

'I neither accepted nor refused the invitation.' Hannah crossed her arms and glared. 'I'm refusing it now.' She sent a quick thank-you to the gods of common sense for coming to her rescue. 'Am I being clear enough?'

'Oh, yeah, don't worry. I won't bother you again.'

'Until you come around pleading for me to sell you the house, I assume?' she needled.

'I won't be. I'm through with the whole mess,' Jake declared. 'Satisfied?'

Hannah watched, speechless, as he turned away and strode off back to his house.

14

Jake pulled out one of the kitchen chairs and collapsed onto it, allowing his head to drop forward on his folded arms. He'd tossed out to Hannah his promise of being through with the spa project in a wave of frustration, but she hadn't exactly thrown herself at him in joyful gratitude. Mikkel would be ruthless if he tried to weasel out of the job, and Hannah wouldn't talk to him again if he backed down. Either way, he was done for. He couldn't even begin to consider the list of all the other people mad at him.

He got up and dragged himself up the stairs to his bedroom to get changed. After putting on a pair of black wool slacks and a matching cashmere sweater, he tried to tug a comb through his tangled curls, but gave up. Without bothering to search for a pair of clean socks, he slipped on a pair of black loafers and headed back downstairs.

The five-minute drive was his only breathing space, so he'd better turn his brain on fast. As he brought his battered old truck to a stop outside Polkirt House, he couldn't help smiling at the contrast with his stepfather's gleaming black Mercedes.

'*God aften*, my dear.' Jake's mother strolled out from the house and he submitted to her warm embrace, wishing her good evening in return.

'You're looking lovely tonight.' It wasn't a lie, because she'd retained her good looks, and with her subtle make-up, elegant clothes, and maybe a few shots of Botox, could pass for at least a decade younger than her fifty-five years.

Jake dropped his hands away from her shoulders as his stepfather appeared in the doorway. He was sure his mother had married Mikkel for financial security, because he couldn't see what the attraction could be otherwise. To a lonely woman left almost penniless with a son to raise, the wealthy businessman must've seemed heaven-sent.

'Janik. Your mother told me you were unwell at lunch. We are pleased you have recovered.'

Jake caught his mother's brief head-shake behind her husband's back, indicating she'd told one of her rare lies on his behalf. 'Thank you, I'm fine,' he said.

'Come to my office now and we will talk before we eat,' Mikkel ordered, and gave Elsa a bland smile. 'I'm sure you have things to see to in the kitchen. We won't hold you up.' The dismissal was nothing but an excuse, because they all knew the cook would be in charge as usual.

Jake trailed into the house behind them both and followed his stepfather through the hall and into the wood-panelled library he'd earmarked for his office. 'We do not need to be disturbed. Turn off your phone.' Mikkel slammed the door shut behind them and his fake smile disappeared.

Jake took out his mobile and followed instructions before tossing it on the desk. It knocked over a stack of papers but he made no attempt to set them right. Mikkel's jaw tightened, although he didn't say a word. One point to Jake. He resented the fact that his stepfather always brought out his childish side.

'Drink?' Mikkel offered, and Jake knew the cut-crystal decanter held the finest whisky money could buy. His stepfather never drank the stuff himself and still preferred the bottled Danish beer he'd grown up on.

'*Nej tak*,' he refused with as much politeness as he could manage.

'Sit.'

Jake ignored him and held out the folder he'd brought. 'Things have changed since I wrapped this up last night.'

Mikkel slowly made his way back behind the imposing oak desk and settled himself in the red leather chair. He retrieved a case from his pocket, removed a pair of heavy black-rimmed reading glasses, and slipped them on. Finally he started to flip through the report. Making people wait was one of his favourite tricks.

'There's one new condition,' Jake said bluntly.

'Condition?' Mikkel frowned. 'Who are you to give conditions?'

'If I'm to carry on with this job, it must be out in the open,' he hurried on. 'We have to announce our intentions locally and get on with the formalities regarding the planning application. We will decide whether to press forward or not depending on the reactions we receive. I'm not going to railroad this through.'

'You will do what you are told.' Mikkel slammed the folder shut and tossed it down on the desk.

'Or what?'

'Do I need to spell it out, Janik?' The visible pulse in his stepfather's thick neck was the only hint of his true feelings.

'Yeah, go ahead. I'm tired of playing games. How about we call my mother in to listen?' Jake steeled himself not to flinch as Mikkel thumped the desk and

144

fixed his cold, dark eyes on him.

'You will leave Elsa out of this,' he hissed. 'She has had enough trouble from you.'

'Yeah? And whose fault is that? If I hadn't been forced into working for you in the first place, I'd never have ended up accused of — '

The phone jangled; Mikkel snatched it up and barked out his name. After a few minutes he finished the call and glared at Jake. 'One of Pedersen's men has been asking questions in the Green Dragon.'

'How do you know?'

'I keep my finger on everything. You should know this by now,' Mikkel said with chilling sureness. 'Someone calls me if they hear things of interest. It is also how I discovered that you and Miss Hannah Green have been conducting a little romance.'

Jake dug his fingers into his thighs and refused to react. He'd fallen for his stepfather's games one too many times as a younger, more volatile man, but he wouldn't do it again.

A distasteful smile crept across Mikkel's face. 'Your silence tells me all I need to know. My contact heard a conversation last night between Miss Green, your barman friend, and several customers. I understand it ended with her revealing your part in the property sales, and got a negative reaction.'

'Yeah, so what?' Jake's heart thumped as he fought to sound unconcerned.

Mikkel leaned forward. 'You force us to act faster.'

'My report — '

'Is useless now,' his stepfather cut him off. 'You will see Miss Green and offer whatever it takes to acquire her house. Afterwards, we get the planning process started and spread good publicity around the village.' Mikkel pushed his chair back and stood up. 'If you do this, I will consider calling our agreement complete.'

Yeah, like I've any reason to believe you.

His stepfather's eyes darkened. 'You

do not believe me, *søn*. Your mother would be disappointed.'

Jake straightened back his shoulders and clasped his hands loosely in front of him. The simple action made Mikkel take a quick step backwards. His stepfather's short, slight physique made him intimidated by his stepson's size and was a handy weapon to employ in their ongoing battle. 'Hannah may tell me to clear off.'

'I do not think so,' he said dismissively. 'For some reason women find you appealing.'

Jake held his tongue. He would have to reason with Hannah. She wanted to sell, and he guessed she needed the money, so it should be a win-win situation all around. *Doesn't get past the fact that she'll say you lied to her in the first place*. He concentrated his focus on the man now staring him down. 'I don't intend to work for you anymore after this, and I want all the papers you have concerning Aaron Montego's death placed in my possession.'

His stepfather's coarse laughter filled the room. 'As you English say, at last the worm has turned.' Mikkel thrust his hand out and Jake hesitated, not trusting the man an inch but having little choice. 'Deal?'

He shook the hand of his nemesis, still full of doubt. If he could pull this off, he'd be free to clear his name and chart his own path. He had to push aside the fact he couldn't have Hannah as well. Whatever happened, she was lost to him, so what did it matter? By the time she realized he'd charmed his way back into her graces for his own ends, any hope of a relationship between them would be shredded into tiny pieces.

'I do believe it is supper time.' Mikkel headed towards the door.

The idea of eating turned Jake's stomach, but he needed to fake an appetite for his mother's sake. He flinched as his stepfather touched his arm.

'I love her. I would do anything for her.'

Jake searched for any hint of a lie in

the other man's countenance, but found nothing. 'You'd better,' he snapped, and pulled away. Mikkel left the room, and Jake waited a couple of minutes before following.

He'd get through the meal and then prepare to face the woman who'd made him want something he suspected he would never have: an honest, loving relationship. He would have to turn on the 'Jake the Rake' charm again. The one thing he couldn't afford to do was to let himself think too much.

15

Hannah stretched out in the bed and pulled the quilt up around her cold shoulders. Although daylight seeped through the worn blue curtains, she wasn't inclined to move. This was when it would be nice to have a man around to bring her a cup of coffee. *Did Carlton Fenway do anything for you?* He'd clicked his fingers and she'd come running like a prize fool. It wasn't happening again. She'd get her own coffee.

A faint banging noise startled her and she clutched the bedcovers tighter before telling herself not to be stupid. She sat up and listened more closely. The sounds weren't coming from inside the house, so she crept out of the bed and tiptoed over to peep out through a gap in the curtains.

The sight of Jake, stripped to the waist and digging up the broken paving stones, made her forget everything else. The man was right when he said he had ice for blood, but he also had spectacular muscles and the sort of deep tan only achieved by working outside in all weathers.

He's a liar. You don't need another one of those. Hannah refused to keep staring like a love-struck teenager, so she made herself turn away. *Shower and put some clothes on. Go out and ask him what he thinks he's doing when you've sent him away more than once.* The sensible side of her took control and she headed into the bathroom.

Choosing the right outfit to wear was important, because she needed to send a hands-off message. She selected a dark blue high-necked sweater and fitted grey trousers, ignored her make-up bag, and methodically worked her hair into a single tight plait. Then she slowly made her way downstairs, relieved to know the new carpet would be delivered and fitted tomorrow, lessening her chances of tripping and breaking her neck.

The aroma of fresh coffee lured her towards the kitchen, and as she walked in Hannah spotted a full pot steaming away in the corner. On the counter next to it stood a white paper bag. She could guess what it contained without even opening it — hopefully more of the delicious chocolate croissants Jake had brought her the other day.

'Help yourself, or I'll eat them all. I didn't bother to stop for any breakfast earlier and I'm starved.'

Hannah jerked around and a fierce rush of heat flooded her face. Jake was grinning at her while he tugged on an old blue T-shirt. Her power of speech evaporated.

'Thought you were a talker in the mornings? Guess I was wrong,' he teased, reaching around her to grab the bag and pull out a pastry, which sent flaky crumbs scattering all over the floor. Taking a large bite, he swallowed and flashed her another megawatt smile. 'Pour me a mug, will you?'

Hannah blushed again and knew he

was loving every minute of disconcerting her. 'Of course.' She fetched two mugs out of the cupboard and ordered her hands to remain steady while she poured his first. She didn't trust herself to place it safely in his hands, so set the mug down on the corner of the table and went back to get her own. By the time she had made her coffee and put her own croissant on a plate, Jake was stretched out in one of her kitchen chairs.

'Bring the bag over, sweetheart. One's not gonna hack it.'

'Isn't it rather a girly breakfast to do a lot of hard work on?'

Jake's teasing smile settled on her mouth. 'You offering to cook me up a full English breakfast?'

'Only if it includes grilling you along with the bacon.'

He chuckled and she fought against laughing along with him. 'Someone's sharp this morning. You'll cut yourself if you're not careful, honey.'

'Someone else doesn't understand when they've been told to go away.'

Jake gave an easy shrug. 'Hey, I said I'd help with the garden, and I keep my promises.'

There was so much she wanted to say — that it was unnecessary but appreciated, and that she wasn't going to sell the house no matter how many paths he fixed or weeds he pulled. But the words stuck in her throat as he set his cup down on the table and stared her up and down. 'Come and sit with me,' he invited her.

She chose the chair furthest away from him and settled her breakfast in front of her. To avoid looking at him, she sipped her coffee and took a bite of her heavenly croissant.

'I can't keep the promises I made last night,' Jake said.

'Which one?' A knot formed in her stomach as she glanced up and met his clear eyes, which she saw were full of regret.

'Either. Both. Not bothering you again. It isn't going to happen, because I can't stay away.' The rueful note in his voice almost drew a smile from her. He leaned across and rested his hand against her cheek and she softened into his touch. For a second neither of them moved, their breathing the only sound in the room.

Hannah cleared her throat. 'The other promise?'

'I said I was done with the property buying around here, but I can't get out of this job. I've got to wrap this up, and then I can quit.' He whispered something under his breath that she couldn't quite catch, but thought it might have been the words 'I hope'.

'I suppose you're under contract?'

He nodded. 'It's a tad more complicated, but you don't need the details; they're ugly.'

Hannah hadn't risen to be a successful financial analyst in the City by being a shy, retiring, 'afraid to say boo to a goose' little girl. 'Fine. Go ahead and leave right now. This time you'll stay gone. I'll make sure of it.'

'Or?'

155

'Trust me,' Hannah stated baldly. 'I swore never to allow another man into my life unless he could convince me he was honest.'

'Does flirting with you here in the kitchen count?' Jake's half-hearted attempt at a joke fizzled away.

Hannah nodded and watched his eyes turn cold. She'd lost him. *What did you expect? Deep down he's no different from Carlton.* 'Thank you for all your help, but you won't need to do any more. I won't be selling Rose Cottage, either.'

'And if most people in village decide they want the scheme to go through?' Jake challenged.

'I might be prepared to reconsider.'

He stood up and so did she. Before she could move, he closed the distance between them with a single step and wrapped his arms around her waist. Surrounded by his clean, warm scent, Hannah struggled to think straight. 'We're going public with the idea tomorrow and submitting the planning application,' he told her.

'I suppose we'll see what happens

then, won't we?' she retorted, but Jake didn't reply. 'I told you to go,' she murmured.

'Your words did,' he acknowledged with a smile that barely turned up the edges of his mouth. 'But this didn't.' Hannah was startled as he placed his hand on top of her thumping heart. Tears pricked at her eyes, but she refused to answer, and Jake's hands dropped back down to his sides. 'Fair enough. I won't stay where I'm not wanted.'

He walked away, his bare feet making no sound on the tiled floor. Hannah didn't dare to breathe again until the door closed with a quiet click. Then her hands flew up to her face and she burst into tears.

16

Jake dug furiously, focusing all his attention on the new flowerbeds he was creating for Mrs. Tregrehan. He'd turned off the phone lodged deep in his pocket so that he didn't hear any more calls coming in. As soon as the planning application appeared on the council website yesterday, his phone had started ringing and hadn't stopped since. Listening to the first three messages had told him all he needed to know — the Christiansson Spa Resort wasn't wanted in Polzennor. The fact that Rose Cottage wasn't theirs yet hadn't stopped his stepfather, who had crafted the application to build around it if necessary. Essentially it would leave the house stranded at the end of the road but still accessible, so there was no real way for Hannah to complain. But Jake knew she would.

They hadn't spoken for five days, ten

hours and fifty-five minutes — not that he was counting. He'd seen her going in and out and even opened the front door once to call out to her before telling himself not to be stupid. She'd sent him away and made it clear she wanted nothing more to do with him. He couldn't blame her for not trusting him, but it ripped him apart, because he had never wanted to be that sort of man and knew he wasn't deep inside. If there was any way to prove his worth to Hannah, he'd do it in a heartbeat; but everything he thought of ran him right into a brick wall. He had to complete this job and then hope to prove his innocence in Aaron Montego's death. Maybe afterwards he could get his life back.

He heard footsteps behind him and turned to see Hannah staring at him from the path, her face pale and set. 'I'm just delivering a leaflet to Peggy. Don't let me disturb you.'

He couldn't speak. He didn't know how to do 'polite and friendly' with this woman who'd tangled him up in knots. All he wanted was to kiss her and beg her forgiveness, but he wasn't stupid enough to do either.

She made her way across the lawn towards him and waved a pile of papers in the air. 'These are about the meeting scheduled for tonight. A group of concerned citizens are organizing the local resistance to your boss's building plans.'

'Led by you?' Jake asked, sticking his fork in the soft earth and standing up to face her.

A rush of heat darkened Hannah's skin and he regretted embarrassing her.

'Sorry, none of my business,' he mumbled, and her cynical laughter startled him.

'It most certainly *is* your business. I've already received my personal letter from the council about the planning application, because your new facility will be on my doorstep, and you know it's up on the council website. We get three weeks to submit our written objections before the application goes to be decided on. Because it's a major development and there are objections, it'll go to the strategic planning committee. That's when they'll have to hold a public meeting and we get a chance to speak. We intend to make the most of the opportunity.'

Jake considered asking who 'we' were, but bit his tongue. He'd seen Andy, the non-boyfriend, going in to Rose Cottage more times than he liked; and from Roscoe's coolness every time he went for a pint, he guessed his old friend was another of the ringleaders.

'Would you care for one?' Hannah thrust one of the leaflets in his direction, her eyes glittering with a definite challenge.

'Sure.' As he took the paper from her, their fingers brushed and Hannah jumped back, stumbling on the uneven grass. Jake's hand shot out to stop her from falling and she grasped hold of him. Instinctively pulling her close, he struggled to breathe, soaking up her light floral scent and loving the warmth of her filling his arms. 'Hannah.' He exhaled a heavy sigh. As she glanced up, Jake wanted nothing more than to drown in her sea-green eyes. Her glossy pink lips were only inches away, and he knew how soft they'd be if he kissed her.

'Don't,' she murmured.

'Don't what?'

'Look at me that way,' Hannah pleaded, the rasp in her voice telling him what she wouldn't — that she was equally affected by their nearness.

'What way would that be?' He dared to stroke his fingers down her arm, touching her just enough to make her tremble. Did she realize he was shaking too?

She cleared her throat and gave him an anguished look. 'You know,' Hannah whispered, her simple words almost inaudible. 'I need to go.'

Jake let her loose. 'I'm not stopping you.'

Hannah tried to make her feet move away from the man whose ice-blue eyes were staring her down. She'd done a good job of avoiding him for days, but had known her luck would run out soon. 'I'll see you around.' The banal words were the best she could come up with.

'Not if you can help it, I'm sure.' His cynical reply made her cringe. He turned away and went back to digging.

There was nothing she could say, so Hannah hurried away, almost running back down the road. She needed to finish her self-appointed task and get back to the cottage before the carpet fitters arrived.

A couple of hours later she was soaked to the skin after dragging herself around half the village delivering leaflets and trekking back up the hill. She opened the door to Rose Cottage and sighed with relief as she closed it behind her and started to strip off her wet clothes. Immediately the doorbell rang and she cursed under her breath, tugging her damp shirt back on. Why were workmen early when you didn't want them to be?

She plastered on a smile before opening the door. 'Mother! What are you doing here?' The sight of her mother, immaculate as ever and twenty-four hours early, made her heart sink.

'Not quite the reaction I was hoping for, Hannah, dear.' Her acerbic reply was instantly followed by a guilty look. 'I took a day off work and raced down here because you sounded so . . . upset.'

They always did understatement well. Opening up and being honest wasn't a Green family trait. Hannah knew she should apologise, but was too flustered after her encounter with Jake to think straight.

'Could I possibly come inside, or are you going to leave me standing on the doorstep all day?'

'Of course. Sorry.' She stepped to one side and let Janie walk in past her. Her mother stopped in the middle of the living room and placed her small weekend bag down on the carpet. She stared around, checking out the place with her usual thoroughness. Hannah

164

found she was holding her breath and waiting for the nod of approval. She'd become oddly fond of the house and didn't want her mother's reaction to be the same as her own on that first day.

'It's as I expected — outdated and dreary,' Janie said with a tight half-smile.

'I painted the walls in here a couple of days ago and have given everything a good clean. I'm having new carpet laid this afternoon — in fact, I thought that was who it was when you arrived. There should be a new roof on by the end of next week, and I'm having repairs done to the windows and the outside repainted.' Hannah knew she sounded defensive, but hated to hear her aunt's house so maligned.

'You're doing your best, which is nothing less than I'd expect from you.' Janie's effort to make concessions had little effect on Hannah's confidence. 'It'll make it more attractive to buyers, I'm sure.'

Hannah didn't quite know how to

reply. She wasn't sure she could talk about Jake and the resort plans without giving away her own feelings. The last thing she needed was her mother interfering in an effort to protect her from getting hurt again. Janie would have ripped Carlton Fenway apart if she could have got her hands on him — not that Hannah would have stopped her. In fact, she'd have joined in.

'I was about to make a cup of coffee. Would you like one?'

'Don't you need to change first?' Her mother's gaze swept down over her. 'I have no idea why you're looking like a drowned rat, but you'll catch your death of cold if you stand there with your hair dripping wet much longer.'

The full explanation was too complicated, so Hannah stuck with a simple one of going for a walk and getting caught in a downpour. Later would do for more details. She'd hardly be able to sneak out to the protest meeting without sharing everything with her mother.

'Tell me where the kitchen is and I'll

put the kettle on to boil while you dry off.'

Hannah didn't bother to argue. 'It's over there on the left.' She pointed across the room and hurried off upstairs to do as she'd been told and hopefully gather her wits at the same time.

After a quick hot shower, she slipped on a clean pair of dark jeans and her favourite rose-pink wool jumper. Then she brushed her hair and deftly wound it up in an elegant chignon. She took a few minutes to reapply her make-up and dab a touch of perfume behind her ears. Her mother always looked smart and she didn't want to be at a disadvantage before they even started.

The doorbell rang again, and Hannah was about to hurry downstairs when she remembered the dangerous state of the stairs. She could just imagine the newspaper headline if she broke her neck letting the carpet fitters into the house.

'I'll get it, Mother,' she shouted down, and went to open the door.

'Miss Green?' The young, skinny

man wearing brown overalls two sizes too big for him gave her a shy smile. When she nodded, he turned and beckoned to an older man standing by a delivery van out in the road.

They soon got everything unloaded, and once they were ready to get to work, Hannah told them to come into the kitchen if they needed anything. She left them to it and went to join her mother, but as soon as she took one step into the room she froze. Janie sat at the table with a photo album opened in front of her, sobbing as though her heart would break.

17

Hannah crept over and rested a hand on her mother's shoulder. 'What's wrong?'

'It's been over twenty years. You'd think it would get easier, but it doesn't.' Janie's voice cracked and she slammed the album shut, pushing it so hard it tipped off the edge of the table and crashed to the floor.

Hannah rushed around to pick up the heavy book and set it back on the countertop instead, pushing the photos that came loose back in to sort out later. The two of them weren't often on the same wavelength, but for once Hannah understood her mother. She herself had never got over her father abandoning them, and his early death had only made things worse. It meant she'd never been able to talk to him as an adult and find out why he'd left. Carlton had tapped into her insecurity by making promises she wanted to hear while never intending to keep them. And Jake had the nerve to ask her to trust him? He didn't have a clue. *Maybe because you never told him.*

She made two quick mugs of instant coffee and put in front of her mother before sitting down at the table. Loud banging noises from the other room echoed through the silence in the kitchen, and Hannah guessed the men were starting work on the stairs.

Janie glanced up and rested her sad eyes on Hannah. 'You won't like what I've got to say,' she warned.

'Maybe not, but I still need to hear it.'

Her mother nodded. 'You're right.' She straightened her shoulders and fixed a hard stare on Hannah.

Her heart thumped in her chest. 'Was it Dad's shirt I found?'

Janie shrugged. 'I expect so. He was here enough.'

Things began to click into place. 'Before he left us?'

'Before, during and after,' her mother said bitterly. 'I'm going to say this once, and we will never talk about it again. Do I make myself clear?' All Hannah could do was nod. 'We all went to the local secondary school in St. Austell, and I'd noticed your father, but he was two years ahead of me and didn't know I existed. I drove Betsy crazy mooning over him for months, and dragged her along with me to a school disco one Saturday night.' Her voice softened. 'He asked me to dance. I couldn't believe it.'

Hannah couldn't take her eyes off her mother's shining eyes. The story continued and she tried hard to hang on to the nice parts. Kevin Green swept Janie off her feet and persuaded her to leave school at sixteen so they could marry and move to London, where he'd been offered a job. 'What did you want to do before he came along?' She'd never thought of her mother as having her own ambitions before, but supposed she must have done.

'I was all set to go on to the sixth form and then on to university. I loved history and wanted to teach.'

'Really?'

'Yes, really.' The sharp reply left no doubt in Hannah's mind that she'd offended her. 'Being a shop assistant for all these years wasn't in my plans, I can assure you.' Hannah kept quiet and let her mother carry on. 'We were too young, and once the initial excitement wore off I complained a lot, I know I did. I wanted to go out and have fun, but we didn't have enough money. I got pregnant almost right away and had you, so Kevin needed to work long hours to support us. It . . . drove us apart.' Her mother reached over and touched her hand. 'It wasn't your fault. Don't you go thinking that.'

Hannah tried to dredge up a smile, but it was a struggle. It was such an ordinary story, but with huge implications. A man unappreciated at home seeks comfort from an understanding woman, and before they know it things

172

go into freefall and everything shatters. 'When did you find out?' she asked.

Her mother took a sip of coffee before answering. 'I knew something was up, but was too scared to bring it out into the open. Betsy never seemed to keep boyfriends long, but I assumed she hadn't met the right one yet.'

She'd met the right one all right, but couldn't have him. It must run in the family.

'Betsy used to come up for the weekend at least once every month, and several times I came across your father and her talking and laughing together, but never thought anything of it. I was pleased they got on well.'

'Was it at my party that you realized what had been happening?'

'Yes,' Janie whispered. 'I saw him kissing her in the garden. I told myself he'd had a couple of beers, but she didn't push him away. I confronted them both and they admitted they'd been close for while. They said they'd tried to fight it,' she scoffed.

'Maybe they did.' Hannah wanted to believe it hadn't been an easy choice.

'I didn't deserve that from either of them.'

Her mother was right. Nothing excused their behaviour. 'No, you didn't.'

'Thank you. I've always thought you blamed me. I had my faults.' She smiled. 'Still do. But it was still wrong.'

Hannah couldn't argue with her mother's statement. The banging continued and she wished the men would hurry up and finish.

'I lost my husband as well as my sister.' Janie's quiet words sliced right through Hannah. 'To be honest, I'm not sure which was worse. Betsy and I were so close growing up, and I missed her terribly.'

Hannah tried to find something comforting to say. 'If it's any consolation, I'm sure she missed you too. I get the impression from talking to people here that she changed after I stopped coming. She became something of a recluse and lost interest in the house and garden.'

174

Janie managed a wan smile. 'That's obvious, looking around the place.'

Glancing up at the clock, Hannah realized she'd better get on with broaching the subject of the planning objection meeting. Her mother would think she was mad, but that was the least of her worries.

'Um . . . there's something going on in the village that I've sort of got mixed up in.' Before Janie could start questioning her, she launched into the whole story minus her personal involvement with Jake. 'That's it, really,' she concluded with a sigh.

'Quite enough, I would think.' Janie shook her head in disbelief. 'For goodness sake, Hannah, be sensible for a change. You need money, and you're being offered a golden opportunity here. Maybe you can make enough to set yourself up in a little business, or travel, whatever you like.' She fixed her daughter with a hard stare. 'Don't be a fool again.'

The whole sorry mess she'd made of

her life hit Hannah with a vengeance, and she bit back tears.

'I don't mean to be cruel, but I've had it hard all these years and don't want the same for you,' her mother continued. 'It wasn't easy bringing you up alone, and I was so happy when you did well at university and in your job.' Her face softened. 'It seemed all the sacrifices were worthwhile, and it broke my heart to see you treated so badly by that awful man and your bank.' She gave Hannah's hand a tentative pat.

The unfamiliar gesture from her undemonstrative mother broke Hannah's self-control, and she burst into tears.

'It's all right, love,' Janie murmured, and came around the table to hug her. Hannah stiffened, but her mother held on, and as her familiar lily-of-the-valley scent trickled into Hannah's awareness, something inside her softened. They stayed in each other's arms for several minutes before moving apart. 'If you insist on going through with this, I'll support you, but I'd recommend you

176

think carefully.' Janie frowned and Hannah wished she could wipe the worry away. Presumably that was what being a parent was all about — teaching, giving advice, and then sitting back while your children made their own decisions, right or wrong.

'I understand your reasoning, Mum, but I have to do this. It feels right. I always loved it here, and don't want to see the heart ripped out of the village.' Putting her feelings into words lifted a weight from her heart, and for the first time in days a comforting sense of calm came over her.

The young carpet fitter poked his head in around the door and grinned. 'Miss Green, we're done. You want to come and have a look?'

'I certainly do.' She hurried to follow him back in to see the stairs. 'Oh, what a difference it makes.' The new tweed carpet, a pretty dark green and beige weave, looked so good that it made up her mind. 'When you get back to the shop, tell your boss I'd like this room done with the same carpet. Maybe you can measure it up now?' she asked the older man.

'No probs.' He got out his metal tape measure and gestured to the boy to help.

'Are you sure, dear?' Janie asked, and Hannah tossed a bright smile right at her mother.

'Absolutely.' It was the surest she'd been of anything in a long time.

* * *

Jake knew this was probably a mistake, but after seeing Hannah earlier he'd made up his mind to go to the meeting. He wasn't going to hide anymore. If Mikkel found out, he'd be furious — make that *when* he found out, because he'd be sure to have spies out tonight.

There was no point wearing his usual gardener's attire because he'd only be mocked, Jake mused, so he picked out clean chinos and a blue shirt. His hair was a mess and he tried to remember the last time he'd had it cut. It must've been back in the spring. Now the best he could do was drag a comb through it and leave it damp. Hopefully it wouldn't dry too fast and turn him into a Scandinavian yeti.

He checked his watch. If he strolled down the hill now, he should be able to slip into the back of the room with the meeting already started, and lessen the awkwardness factor.

Fifteen minutes later he stood outside the church hall and listened to the buzz of angry voices drifting out. He sucked in a deep breath and opened the door. Instantly several people in the back row turned and glared at him. He watched in silence as the news spread by a series of whispered conversations and nudges.

Jake glanced towards the woman speaking into the microphone on the stage, who he suddenly realized was Hannah. As she met his eyes, all the colour leached from her face.

18

Hannah reminded herself to breathe. She stared back down at her notes and tried to look as though she was thinking. Instead of making her next point to the assembled crowd, she was consumed by how handsome Jake looked tonight. That idea was mixed with a burning desire to yell at him and ask what on earth he was doing here. She caught her mother watching her, and it was obvious from her piercing stare that Janie knew something was up but didn't know what it was yet.

Straightening her shoulders, Hannah pulled herself together. 'Right. Andy will write the main points that we need to put in the objection letters up on the board.' She gestured towards her friend who was standing nearby with a marker in his hand. 'We need to get these letters in the post as soon as possible.

On the flyers we've handed out, you'll find the address to send them to, and also the email address if you prefer to send your objections that way.' She threw Jake a challenging fake smile. 'Mr. Walton, we didn't expect the pleasure of your company tonight.' His eyes narrowed. 'Would you be prepared to answer any questions we have about your company's plans?' Let him get out of that.

'I'm not here in an official capacity, but as long as that's understood I'm happy to share my views,' he replied, with no hint that she'd managed to rattle him.

Hannah nodded. 'I'm sure we'd be grateful.' The edge to her voice should send the message that gratitude wasn't the primary emotion being felt here. 'Would you care to come to the stage so you can use the microphone?'

A brief flicker of annoyance crossed Jake's face, but he politely accepted her offer and started to make his way down the aisle towards her. As he leaped up the couple of steps and came to stand next to her, Hannah swallowed hard, struggling to keep her composure. His hair gleamed under the lights and she became far too aware of the fresh, clean scent she always associated with him.

She passed over the microphone with her fingertips so she wouldn't touch him, but he swept it out of her hand, brushing his warm skin against hers. Her cheeks burned, and she caught a hint of mischief in the turned-up edges of his mouth. She moved to stand next to Andy, and was reassured when he gave her a friendly nod.

'Good evening. I appreciate y'all giving me the opportunity to butt in on your meeting.' Jake's ease took Hannah by surprise, although it really shouldn't have. There was always an easy confidence about him that was very appealing. He proceeded to run through the plans and emphasized the benefits for the village. There was little emotion running through his descriptions, and it made Hannah wonder what he *really* thought about the resort. For the next half-hour he fielded questions, giving very little away they didn't already know. Hannah sensed some of the audience wavering in their opinions and wondered if she'd made a big mistake offering him the chance to speak.

Andy poked her in the ribs. 'Wake up, Snow White. He's offering you back the mic.'

From what Hannah remembered, the woman in question was woken from her sleep with a kiss from a handsome prince. Well, Jake was no prince, and he'd better not have any such thing in mind. She met his sparkling eyes and knew he'd overheard Andy's comment. The annoying man always knew exactly what she was thinking.

She took the microphone and managed to thank him, although it just about killed her. He left the stage and returned to his place at the back of the room, where he leaned back against the wall, fixed his attention on her, and gave a long, slow wink.

That was mean. Yeah, but she was

mean to you too. Jake convinced himself he hadn't been *too* unkind. While the meeting continued, he scanned the room, interested to note who was and wasn't there. He'd like to work out who Mikkel's contact was at the pub, because he'd bet anything the same person would be here tonight ready to report back. It must be someone who either worked in the Green Dragon or was a regular drinker there. Roscoe was out. Jake considered he was a good enough judge of character to recognize an honest man when he met one, and his friend's love for his home village ran deep. The half-dozen or so men who routinely propped up the bar were all locals, and he couldn't imagine any of them giving his stepfather the time of day. Jake thought about Pete Tregunna, the landlord, but he was a grouchy old so-and-so and rarely spoke to anyone more than he had to. That left the other bar staff, all of them part-time, and who changed according to the season and how busy it was.

His gaze rested on Maddie Truscott,

sprawled in a chair near the front. She was checking out her nails and fiddling with her phone at the same time. After two long, boring dates, Jake had concluded that no matter how pretty she was, nothing could make up for her conversational skills, which were limited to inane celebrity gossip and the latest fashions. He couldn't imagine why she'd bothered to come, because he would have thought she'd approve of more tourists flashing their money around Polzennor. He watched her angle her phone towards the stage as if to take a picture, and a chill ran through him. It was time to offer Maddie the drink he'd promised her weeks ago.

As the meeting started to break up, some people hung around to chat, and Jake waited for his moment. He eased away from the wall as Maddie headed his way, and flashed one of the smiles he'd been told could charm the birds from the trees. Tonight he only needed to tempt one little cuckoo. 'Hi, gorgeous,' he said. Maddie flushed and shoved her phone in her pocket. 'Fancy a drink?'

A sly smile crept across her face. 'I'm supposed to go straight home to babysit my little brother, but I might be persuaded if it's not in the Dragon.' She played with the ends of her long black hair. 'That place is for old people, and I see enough of it working there.'

'Sounds good to me, sweetheart.' Jake slipped his arm around her shoulder and steered her out through the door. 'How about we go to the Ring O' Bells instead?' He hated the place with a passion, but would endure a couple of hours there to find out what he needed to know.

'Sure.' Maddie wound her arms around his waist and gazed up at him through fake eyelashes that were long enough to sweep the floor. She launched into a story all about a pop singer Jake had never heard of; he was only saved when her phone started to buzz. Retrieving it from her pocket, she glanced at the screen, then at him, and a hot blush crept up to flood her face. 'It's my Mum.' She scanned the incoming text and tapped back a reply.

Mikkel. Next time choose a better liar to do your dirty tricks. Jake waited patiently while the back-and-forth texts went on until Maddie shoved the phone away again.

'Sorry, handsome, but I've got to go home. My mum's waiting to go out and she's cross.' She grimaced and reached up to pop a kiss on his cheek. As she flounced off down the road, Jake breathed a sigh of relief. People always ran when Christiansson snapped his fingers. If she was supposed to go and report straight after the meeting, then that was what she'd better do, otherwise she'd be in bigger trouble than she could imagine.

Jake hesitated, then decided against going for a drink. Returning home was the wiser option. He wasn't in the mood for any more interrogations tonight.

* * *

'So, are you going to tell me who the Norse god is? After you've done that, you can explain why you lit up like a fire engine when he looked at you. As if I couldn't guess.' Her mother's sharp words made Hannah wince. Just because she'd known the questions were coming didn't make answering them any easier. They were supposed to be joining everyone in the pub, but Janie had pulled Hannah to one side before they even got out of the church hall. Hannah shifted from one foot to the other and wracked her brains for a reasonable explanation. *There isn't one, silly.*

'He's my neighbour. His name is Jake Walton. At least, that's the name he's using around the village.'

'You make it sound as though he's an undercover agent,' Janie said with a disbelieving laugh.

'He sort of is.' Hannah rushed on to get it over with. 'He works as a gardener, but he's really a half-Danish/half-American property developer called Janik Eriksen. Jake's been secretly buying up properties on behalf of a client who wants to build the spa resort we were discussing tonight.' Her mother gave her shrewd look and Hannah's cheeks flamed. 'He, um, helped me out when I arrived.'

'I'm sure he did.' Janie's dry comment added to the tension humming between them.

'Before you say any more, yes I was attracted to him, but I sent him away.' *Twice, but he keeps coming back.* 'I want nothing to do with a man who isn't absolutely upfront with me. I can't trust him.' Hannah's voice broke and she stared down at her feet — anything so that she didn't have to see the concern in her mother's eyes.

'I suggest you remember that the next time he flutters those killer blond eyelashes in your direction.'

Hannah almost made a joke about the fact Janie had noticed them too, but decided discretion might be wiser at this point. 'Would you mind if we skipped going to the pub? I'd rather go straight home. It's been a long day.' Plus, she didn't want to risk bumping into Jake and the sharp-tongued young barmaid she'd seen him sloping off with. For some reason, the sight of them together disappointed her, and she didn't care to think it was because she was jealous. *Not much, it isn't.*

'It has for me too,' Janie said. 'Let's go.'

They turned around to head in the opposite direction from the beachfront. The silence between them as they strolled along was a comfortable one, and Hannah couldn't remember the last time that had been the case. Despite the Jake problem, coming to Cornwall hadn't been a complete mistake on her part. For the first time in a couple of years she embraced a sense of optimism, and liked how that made her feel.

Hannah linked her arm with her mother's as they walked together up the hill, and caught Janie's surprised smile. Definitely a good decision.

19

Jake sprawled on his recliner out on the patio, half-asleep, knowing he should go on to bed but not caring how tired he'd be tomorrow. He'd received another of his stepfather's impatient texts ordering him to present himself at the house at eight in the morning. Mikkel didn't bother asking if Jake had any other jobs scheduled, and it didn't take a genius to guess he was in for a dressing-down. *Just for a change.*

He glanced across the garden and noticed the lights go out in one of the bedrooms. It wasn't Hannah's corner room, so must be her guest. The woman he'd seen her with at the meeting must be her mother — one glance at her elegant figure and pale green eyes told him that. Jake had caught her checking him out while he was speaking and would bet a hundred-dollar bill that Hannah got interrogated about him afterwards. He idly wondered how she'd replied, and guessed it'd probably be something on the lines of him being a helpful neighbour who'd proved himself to be only after her house. Jake was pretty sure she wouldn't mention how much she enjoyed his kisses.

The memories of holding Hannah in his arms sent a shiver running through him and he jumped up off the chair. *Get to bed and stop being an idiot.*

'I swear you'd still be out here half-dressed if there was snow on the ground.' Hannah's teasing voice stopped him where he was and he slowly turned around. Her wary smile peeking at him over the top of the hedge made him ache to kiss her all over again.

'Half-dressed?' He glanced down over his jeans and T-shirt, then at her. 'I suppose compared to your arctic gear it is.' The thick red coat she wore over a pair of blue flannel pyjamas seemed overkill to him.

She bit her lip and didn't say anything.

'Did you decide to admire your garden in the dark?' Jake wanted to make her admit she had come out because he was there.

'Is Maddie not with you?' She ignored his question, and he stifled a smile.

'Nope.' He only debated for a few seconds. It was time for some truth between them. He wandered over closer. 'I don't know for sure, but I think she's been keeping her ears open around the village and reporting back to my boss. He always knows what's going on.' *Including all about us.* 'Before tonight I didn't know who he was using as a spy, but she pretty much confirmed it by being there. Maddie doesn't give a toss about stopping the resort being built. She'd love nothing better than an influx of wealthy visitors. Probably get herself a job there.'

'I was surprised to see you at the meeting too,' Hannah declared, a flush of heat colouring her cheeks.

'Good.'

She raised her eyebrows at him. 'Why?'

'Because I want you to see I'm not a monster, Hannah. I'm just doing my job. I don't like the secretive side of these projects, but that's the nature of the beast.' He wanted to explain himself more but could only go so far. Why he was working for Christiansson in the first place wasn't for her ears. 'If we'd brought everything out in the open from day one, our competitors would have beaten us to it. That's what this business is like, honey.'

Monster? She'd never called him that. 'I'm not stupid. I understand. But . . .' Hannah stumbled over her words, unable to explain her feelings without sharing too much.

'I get that you're wary. I know that Fenway idiot messed you around. This wasn't ever personal.'

'It is to me,' Hannah snapped. 'That's what you don't see. I don't care if you misled the whole village.' She backtracked in a hurry. 'Sorry, I didn't mean that. Now I sound totally selfish.'

Jake shushed her. 'Don't. You're a

good person.' He leaned over the hedge, so close she could have reached out and touched him. But she didn't. 'Does your mother know you're out here consorting with the enemy?' He flashed a quick grin when she couldn't hide her surprise. 'You look so much like her, it was obvious.'

'She went on to bed,' Hannah explained with a shrug.

'You fancy a beer?'

She shook her head. 'Better not.'

'You're probably right.'

I don't want to be. 'What's your next move in all this?' Hannah asked, not expecting a very honest answer. This was business. He'd just told her that.

'I meet my boss tomorrow morning and we'll go through our publicity strategy. I'm sure I'll be designated to try to swing more of the locals over to our side.'

'And are you happy to do that? Do you really believe it's best for this area?' Hannah plugged on. Something about Jake's willingness to go along with this didn't work for her. Maybe he was doing this for the money and there was nothing more to it. *Do you just not want to believe it?*

'I can see the advantages. Can we leave it at that?' he pleaded.

Before she could answer, her mother's voice drifted out from the house. 'Hannah? Where are you?'

'Out here. I'm coming. Put the kettle on,' she called back over her shoulder, and shrugged at Jake. 'Sorry,' she whispered. 'Got to go.'

He suddenly grasped her hand. 'Don't believe everything you hear. All right?'

Somehow Hannah managed to nod, not really understanding his question but knowing it was important to him. Jake brushed his lips over her fingers and she trembled. With a sad smile he let go and walked away. She took several deep, steadying breaths before doing the same.

'What on earth were you doing outside at this time of night?' her mother chided from the kitchen doorway. 'You'll catch your death of cold.'

Hannah smiled. She'd said exactly the same to Jake. 'I needed some fresh air.'

'You got plenty of that, I should think. It's freezing,' Janie declared, and stepped back inside with an exaggerated shiver.

'I'm trying not to be such a townie.'

Her mother scoffed, 'You're London born and bred. Don't tell me you've taken to the country life all of a sudden.'

There was a lot Hannah had taken to here, most of which it was wiser not to mention. 'It's better than I expected.' Lame, but borderline honest. She hurried over to stick the kettle on in an effort to distract her mother. 'I'm having chamomile tea. It's too late for coffee.'

'Did I hear you talking out there? You know what they say about talking to yourself.'

The woman was relentless. A hot drink wasn't going to distract her from subjecting her only child to an inquisition worthy of the KGB. Letting her mother think she was a touch crazy was better than admitting the truth. 'Don't fuss. I'm fine.'

Five minutes later they sat across the kitchen table from each other, sipping their drinks and not speaking.

'I came down because I couldn't sleep.'

Hannah met her mother's tired eyes and blinked back tears. Now she regretted being so short with her, but it was the way they'd been for so long it was hard to get out of the habit. 'Sorry.'

'It's being here.' Janie gestured around the room. 'Surrounded by all Betsy's things. It's bringing everything back.' She got up and walked over to the sink, then reached up over it to lift down a small, battered metal biscuit tin from the shelf. 'These Cadbury's Fingers were always her favourites.'

'Did she ever apologize?'

'She tried once or twice right afterwards, but I wouldn't listen.'

Hannah couldn't imagine her mother's pain. She didn't have any brothers or sisters, but felt sure it would hurt terribly to be estranged from them. Nothing would bring back the father she'd adored, or put her family back together. Some things were priceless. If nothing else, Carlton Fenway made her see that. 'It's a shame, but that's all in the past now.'

'That's not the point.'

Hannah reached over and covered her mother's hand with her own. 'Yes, it is. I'm trying to let go of the difficult things that have happened. I don't want to spend the rest of my life bitter over things which can't be changed.'

'It's easier said than done,' Janie said with a sad half-smile.

'Have you tried?' She regretted the words as soon as they left her mouth, but before she could apologize her mother pulled her hand away and stood up.

'I can't believe you would ask me that, after all I've — '

'Done for me,' Hannah finished the sentence. 'I know. You told me often enough.'

Janie shook her head. 'Did I really say that a lot?'

The whispered question tore at Hannah, and she wished she could wind back the clock. She shrugged, unable to lie, but unwilling to hurt her mother any more.

'I'm guessing the answer is yes,' Janie persisted, and Hannah tried not to smile, but in the end was forced to.

'Well, you did, rather. It was usually when I'd been my usual obnoxious self, broken my curfew yet again or given you a mouthful of cheek.'

'So in other words, you deserved it.' The twinkle was back in Janie's eyes.

'Pretty much,' Hannah admitted with a broad grin.

'I think it's time we both went to bed.'

'You go on. I need to lock up.' She shooed her mother away.

Alone again, Hannah didn't hurry. It'd been quite a day, and she had a lot to process before her mind would quieten enough to rest. Jake. The meeting. Her mother. Jake. Why did the man keep popping back in?

She settled in for a long night of thinking.

20

Jake tuned out his stepfather, who would stop ranting soon when he realized he wasn't getting any response. It pleased him to know he'd been right about Maddie. The gullible woman had completely fallen for the spin Mikkel had put on the resort plans. If she wasn't so annoying, Jake thought he might even feel sorry for her.

'Split the opposition. It's the only way we'll succeed.'

He made himself listen. What did the man think he was going to do? People liked him here — at least, they had — and Jake hated the idea of them thinking less of him.

'And do not give me any of your nonsense about morals and business ethics.' Mikkel's blunt statement made Jake wince. 'You managed to overlook those when I saved you from prison.'

Jake wanted to protest that he'd been young and frightened but knew it wouldn't wash. Someone had killed Aaron Montego, and he'd got the blame. He had his suspicions, but if they were right and he proved them, his mother would never forgive him. 'What do you want me to do?' Jake said with a heavy sigh.

Mikkel started to drone on about getting glossy posters and leaflets made promoting the spa. They needed to emphasize the financial benefits to a village struggling for year-round survival on the proceeds of a few months' income from the fair-weather tourists. 'You have to make clear the fact the opponents to the plan aren't thinking of the rest of the village. The ringleaders are all people with jobs, money or both who can afford to do without this development.'

It wasn't true, but Jake held his tongue.

'I hear the Green woman was smiling over you at the meeting. Use it. Take her out and treat her well. A fancy meal. A nice piece of jewellery. Women aren't hard to impress if you are a smart man.'

Jake itched to wipe the satisfied expression from his stepfather's face. One word to his mother and this would all stop. But he immediately berated himself for even thinking that way, because she'd been through enough already. 'I don't intend to use my . . . friendship with Hannah,' he snapped, and waited for the comeback. Mikkel's dark eyes narrowed, but he didn't reply for a minute.

'Fine. How about Mr. Roscoe Burton? He was happy to take our money for his house. What right does he have to argue against it now?'

'But he didn't know about the project then,' Jake protested.

A sly smile crept across his stepfather's face. 'You might think that, but as far as other people are concerned, how can they be sure? It is well known that you and Mr. Burton are good friends, and then he profits from a business you are involved in. It does not look good for him.'

Jake didn't reply, so Mikkel carried right on.

'I appreciate how sensitive you are, so I will get someone else to spread that particular rumour.' The heavy sarcasm rolled right over Jake. 'That silly little girl who works at the pub will do anything for more money.' He fiddled with his heavy gold wristwatch.

Jake dug his fingers into his thighs and waited for what was coming next. No way would he get off this lightly.

'I believe that Mr. Andrew Wareham needs to be your target,' Mikkel pronounced with an air of satisfaction. 'You will find out his weak spot. Everybody has one.'

The idea of making friends with the man didn't cheer Jake up. Hannah could deny it as much as she liked, but it was easy for one man to pick up on another's interest in the woman he . . . *Don't go there*. He'd have to agree to this in order to get Mikkel off his back. It was the lesser of the three evils. 'Fine. I'll see what I can do.'

'Don't take too long. I have other feelers out and will update you as I see fit. I am taking one of the local council-men to lunch today to do my part.'

Jake didn't bother to ask if that would be considered a conflict of interest. Mikkel was no doubt doing it for precisely that reason.

'Off you go and dig up turnips.'

Summarily dismissed, Jake made his escape before his stepfather could come up with another bright idea.

* * *

'I have to say, the view's better from your house than mine,' Janie chuckled as Hannah walked up behind her. As she followed her mother's line of sight out of the kitchen window, her cheeks burned. 'He might be the enemy, but he's a handsome one,' her mother declared with a girlish giggle.

Jake had appeared out of nowhere and was digging up the ground over by her apology for a garden shed. Despite the cool air, he was stripped down to a tight black T-shirt so ragged it was more holes than shirt, and khaki shorts.

'I thought you'd be happy if I kept away from men for the next ten years.' Hannah gave her mother a quizzical stare. 'Make up your mind.'

'There's no harm in looking.'

I'm not so sure. 'Maybe.' She turned away before she bored a hole into Jake with her eyes. 'Lunch?'

Janie shook her head. 'My train's at half past twelve and my taxi will be here in a few minutes. I've packed a sandwich to eat on the journey.'

They'd already had a discussion — make that an argument — about why Hannah didn't need to run her mother to the station. In the end she'd conceded because she didn't want to upset the balance of their fragile newfound closeness.

She was startled as the doorbell went and glanced back out to make sure Jake was still hard at work.

'Ask the driver to wait for a minute while I get my bag down,' Janie said, and ran off before Hannah could offer to get it for her.

Hurrying out into the hall, Hannah opened the door, stared at the older man giving her a hesitant smile, and screamed. Her head spun into a dizzy whirl and everything went black.

21

A man's deep voice saying her name snaked into Hannah's awareness, and as she dared to peek Jake stared down at her, his eyes dark with worry. She tried to sit up but he placed his hand on her arm to stop her.

'Just lie there,' he ordered and she didn't have the strength to argue.

'Why am I on the sofa?'

A gentle smile spread over his face. 'Maybe because that's where I put you after you fainted. I was working in the garden, and . . . um, heard you.' His warm touch soothed the panic pulling at the edge of her brain. *Janie.* 'Where's my mum?'

Jake pulled a soft blanket up over her and tucked it in around her sides. 'You're shivering.'

Hannah glared. 'Jake Walton, or whatever you're calling yourself today, answer me. If you don't tell me, I'll get up and go find out for myself.'

'Fine.' He exhaled a heavy sigh. 'She's in the kitchen with . . . '

The blood froze in Hannah's veins. 'My dad?' Daring to whisper the two words crystallized the bizarre thoughts rattling around her head. 'He's dead. I'm going crazy.'

'No, honey, you're not.' Jake wrapped his arms around her and scooped her up before sitting down and settling her onto his lap. 'I told them I'd call when you came to, but do you want a minute?'

She nodded, unable to speak for the lump filling her throat. The urge to rest her head against his shoulder was overwhelming, and she let her body do what her mind said she shouldn't. For these few moments she wouldn't allow herself to think too much about who or what Jake really was. All she cared about was soaking up his quiet strength so she could face what was coming.

'Hannah, love, are you all right?'

She raised her head and saw her mother standing in the kitchen doorway, looking anxiously in her direction. 'I don't know. Are you going to tell me what's going on?'

Janie sighed. 'It's complicated.'

'Seeing someone come back from the dead usually is, from what I understand.' She couldn't hold back her sarcasm; it was that or burst into tears. 'So make something clear for me. Did I imagine seeing my father a little while ago?'

'No.' Her mother came over and perched on the chair next to Hannah, not quite meeting her eyes.

'You told me he died in a fight.' The blunt comment made Janie wince. 'Was that a lie?'

'How about I go make some tea or coffee while you two talk?' Jake offered, and Hannah couldn't decide whether or not to be grateful. She wasn't sure she wanted to be alone with her mother right now.

'Thank you,' Janie murmured. 'I could do with a cup of tea.'

I could do with a large brandy.

'It'll be okay,' Jake whispered in her ear, then slid her off his lap before disappearing into the kitchen.

'I'm sorry,' Janie said. 'We did what we thought was best.'

Hannah stared at her mother in horror. 'Best? On what planet could it ever be for the best to think my father was dead?' It had been bad enough when he'd left them, but to get the awful news that he'd been killed was devastating.

'It was my idea, poppet.'

All she could do was try to keep breathing, because fainting twice in a matter of minutes would be excessive. Greying at the temples, a little stooped over, and shabbily dressed, an older version of the father she remembered stood in the doorway. He was watching her with a wary look in his sad blue eyes. 'Daddy?' For a second Hannah thought he would be the next one to faint as he grabbed hold of the doorpost for support.

'It was wrong. Very wrong,' Janie

piped up. 'I should never have gone along with it.' A dark flush crept up her neck.

'Do you mind if I sit down?' her father asked.

Hannah couldn't get her head around this tentative man who was a shadow of the charming, good-humoured father she'd adored as a young child. She nodded, and he instantly came over and lowered himself into the chair as if his legs wouldn't hold him up another moment. 'Where do you want me to start?'

There were so many answers she could give, but there were limits to how much she thought she could take. 'I don't want to know why you left us. That's between you and Mum, and frankly I'd rather not hear any details of what happened with you and Aunt Betsy. All I care about is why you two cooked up a lie to make everyone think you'd died.' Hannah had never seen her mother look so uncomfortable.

'I had no close family apart from you and your mum,' he muttered. 'My friends all shunned me when I walked out of my life in Watford.'

Hannah listened to every word, wanting to remember everything so she could go through it in her mind later. Her father carried on, explaining how he knew he'd made a mistake shortly after he left. Betsy was destroyed by what she'd done to her family and sent him away.

'I drifted around and ended up back in London. I worked odd jobs, including one as a night-club bouncer.'

'So there *was* a fight?' Hannah asked, almost relieved.

'Yes, and your dad *was* seriously hurt,' Janie said. 'The hospital called me because they didn't think he was going to pull through.'

'I had nothing to offer you.' Her father's pathetic statement tore at Hannah. 'I suggested to your mum that it'd be better for me to stay out of your life completely. If you thought I was dead, you wouldn't keep asking where I was or why you couldn't see me.' His raspy voice trailed away and it took all Hannah's strength not to reach over and hug him.

She turned on her mother. 'Did you keep in touch all this time? Have you been sending cosy letters and pictures for twenty years? Did you invite him here today for some sort of bizarre family reunion?' She hated the bitterness filling her voice, but couldn't hold back any longer.

'Don't blame Janie,' her father interrupted, and she wanted to tell him he'd given up the right to scold her a long time ago. 'She's always been a fantastic mum, and only did what she thought was best for you.'

Very quietly her mother explained they hadn't kept in touch in any way, and that she'd been as shocked as Hannah when he'd appeared at the door earlier.

'So why *did* you come here?' Hannah persisted, still unable to get today to make any sense.

Janie leaned forward and patted her hand. 'How about we have that cup of tea and talk more later? I think we've all had enough for now.'

Hannah was about to make a sharp reply when she caught sight of Jake standing in the kitchen doorway, holding a tray and shaking his head at her. She'd always been tenacious — or stubborn, depending on people's point of view — but as a wave of tiredness swept through her, she conceded defeat.

He might be an interloper, but Jake hoped that by staying he was helping Hannah. The poor woman didn't know what had hit her, judging by the strain written all across her tight, pale face. He would have a million and one questions too, but her parents didn't look as though they could take much more. 'Here we go.' He quickly set the tray down on the table. 'Coffee, Hannah.' He picked up a mug and placed it in her hands. Straightening up, he turned towards her mother to give one of the smiles his own mother always said nobody could resist. 'Jake Walton. Neighbour and hot-drink specialist.'

Janie Green eyed him up and down. 'We haven't officially met, but I've seen you around, shall we say.'

He nodded and faced the other man, who was now giving him an unfriendly glare. Jake introduced himself again, minus the charming smile this time.

'Kevin Green. I'm Hannah's . . . ' He glanced over at his daughter and Jake suddenly felt sorry for him. How sickening would it feel to wonder if your own child wanted to acknowledge you?

'Jake, this is my father. Dead or alive. Right, Dad?' Hannah tried to make a joke of it, but her voice was strained.

Kevin looked at them both, the wheels obviously turning in his head. It wasn't hard to guess he'd like to question Jake more but didn't feel he had the right.

'Tea or coffee?' Jake asked him.

'Tea. Black. No sugar.' Kevin Green managed a half-smile, and Jake caught a glimpse of the man he must have been before life had thrown him a curveball.

An uneasy silence fell on the room. Jake glanced at Hannah, wondering if he should leave, but she patted the cushion next to her on the sofa. 'Please.'

She'd guessed his intention without him having to spell it out. Jake couldn't begin to question why he wasn't able to turn this woman down. He was supposed to be working his proper job, not digging up Hannah's garden and playing family counsellor.

'So why today . . . Dad?'

Kevin set his mug down on the table and cleared his throat, looking around at them all. Jake knew a cornered man when he saw one.

22

'Did you know we lost Betsy?' Janie interrupted before Hannah's father could speak.

'Yes. It's the reason I'm here.' He shifted in the chair and didn't look directly at anyone. 'I . . . left a few things behind and needed to collect them before the house got sold.'

Waves of tension emanated from him, and Hannah didn't imagine for a moment that he'd come back for a couple of old shirts. 'I've been sorting out a lot of my aunt's things,' she said. 'I hope I haven't thrown away anything you were looking for.' He didn't reply straight away, but gave her mother an embarrassed sideways glance.

'Shouldn't think so. You wouldn't have come across, um, what I'm after,' he mumbled, and Hannah itched to shake him. 'Betsy asked me to hide something the last time I was here, and I promised to retrieve it if anything happened to her.' His voice roughened, and for the first time Hannah felt sorry for him. He must have loved her aunt deeply to risk everything, and had still lost it all in the end. Impulsively she reached over and squeezed his hand. Seeing his tear-filled eyes broke her heart all over again.

'Is it in the garden?' Jake suddenly spoke, and an instant flush heated up her father's cheeks before he gave a long, slow nod of agreement.

'How on earth did you — ' Hannah began, but Jake cut her short.

'Makes sense, honey,' he said kindly. 'Your aunt freaked out when I suggested tidying up the garden, and you've gone through the inside of the house and scrubbed it to within an inch of its life. You'd have found anything else by now.' His logic made complete sense, but she knew she'd never have put it together herself.

'You're all talking in riddles,' Janie

protested. 'I wish someone would tell me what's going on.'

Jake jumped up from the chair. 'You wanna show me where to dig?'

'Dig?' Janie shrieked. 'Don't tell me my sister was stupid enough to bury money in the garden instead of doing up this wreck?' She waved her hands around the room and Hannah bit back a protest.

'It's not only money,' Kevin muttered, and stood up. 'Save the rest of your questions, love.' He gave Jake a grateful smile. 'I'd do it myself, but I'm . . . not quite up to it.'

'What's wrong with you?' Hannah asked.

Her father reached out and stroked her hair. 'My beautiful girl. I'm so glad I got to see you again. It's nothing serious. Haven't been taking good care of myself. Okay?'

'I suppose so.' A sad numbness settled in her stomach. She watched the two men leave the room and couldn't make herself move or say another word.

Jake led the way outside and stopped by the flowerbed he'd been working on to pick up the shovel he'd dropped. 'You gonna tell me where to start, or can we cut to the chase and I'll tell you?' The other man's face paled and he stared at Jake as though he'd grown two heads. 'It was under that rose bush. Right?' He pointed to a dead plant he'd pulled out earlier and tossed to one side, ready to get rid of.

'How the devil did you know?'

Jake squatted in the dirt, reached into the hole where the rose had been, and scrabbled around. 'I hit something metal when I was almost done digging. I was about to investigate when I heard Hannah screaming.' He glanced away to concentrate on pushing the earth around with his fingers, and the only sound was Kevin Green's heavy breathing over his shoulder. Soon he exposed a square black tin and stood back up, holding the battered mud-covered box out to Hannah's father. 'This what you're looking for?' He brushed the worst of the dirt off and passed it into the other man's outstretched hands.

'Yes. Thank you.' The strained words were barely audible.

'You wanna open it out here on your own?' Jake asked, and received a grateful nod. 'Fine.' He knew he should cut his losses and go back to his own house before he got any more involved, but the pain and shock in Hannah's eyes wouldn't let him leave yet. 'See you when you're ready.' He strode off and left Kevin alone. A small remnant of dignity was all the man had left.

Jake nudged off his muddy boots and put them to one side of the step before knocking and walking in through the open door.

'Did you find it, whatever it is?' Hannah pounced on him, and Jake forced himself not to grab hold of her and pull her into a comforting hug. The fact that his hands were caked in mud helped his restraint.

'Yep. Need to wash my hands. Your father will be back in when he's ready.'

In other words, don't pester him. Her face tightened and he knew she'd heard his silent admonition. He headed to the hall bathroom before she could interrogate him. Hannah and holding back didn't go together, but of course that was one of the reasons he loved her.

Loved her? He must be madder than everyone thought. Was that the reason why the idea of leaving Cornwall and Hannah depressed him? Jake turned the tap on full and scrubbed at his filthy hands, picking up the nail brush to finish the job and refusing to consider anything apart from getting all the dirt off. He carefully dried his hands and hung up the towel.

He stepped back into the hall and right up against Hannah, who was standing with her arms folded across her body and glaring at him.

'Tell me exactly what you know.' She didn't mince her words, and he admired her spirit.

'It's nothing much.' He explained about the rose bush and the box. 'I'm thinking y'all might prefer me to go on home. It's family business.' Jake wanted her to disagree but she simply shrugged.

'That might be a good idea, Mr. Walton.' Janie came out from the kitchen, her face grim and unsmiling. 'Thank you for all your help.'

He glanced at Hannah, but if she wanted to argue with her mother she didn't say so. There was nothing else he could do. 'If you need anything, you know where I am. Just call.' She gave a terse nod and went to stand by Janie.

Jake walked past her and headed for the front door. He wasn't sorry to get back outside in the fresh air and took a few deep breaths before strolling down the path. He noticed Kevin kneeling down on the grass with his head bent in over the box, sobbing, but carried on walking.

Hannah let out a slow, deep exhalation and tried to put Jake out of her mind. She'd wanted to grab hold of him and plead for him to stay, but the stubborn side of her refused to need another man for anything.

Suddenly her father flung the door open and stepped back into the house. If she'd thought he looked ill before, any vestige of colour was drained away now. He glanced at them both and sighed. 'We'd better all go and sit down.'

Hannah didn't say a word, but linked her arm with her father's, and they walked together back into the kitchen with her mother trailing after them. After they were settled around the table, no one spoke for a few moments.

With slow deliberation, her father opened the lid of the box in front of him and began to place various things on top of the blue gingham tablecloth she'd bought to cover up the scratched Formica. The last items were three stacks of money secured with rubber bands, which he pushed towards Hannah.

'She wanted you to have this to help with the house.' He gave her a wry smile. 'Betsy distrusted banks.'

I don't blame her. So do I now. 'Thanks,' Hannah murmured. Blowing the dust off, she flipped through and realized they were all fifty-pound notes. At first glance she guessed Betsy had hidden about thirty thousand pounds. 'Why under the rose bush?' It was a random question but didn't appear to surprise her father. His eyes softened and he flashed her mother an apologetic smile.

'I bought it for her thirtieth birthday. It was called Birthday Girl. A cream-edged pink rose with a heady fragrance.' His words trailed away.

'Her birthday was the week after you left us,' Janie said, her voice cold and remote. 'It was the first time I didn't get her a card or present.'

'But not the last,' he said quietly.

She nodded. 'No, not the last.'

'She would have been fifty in a couple of weeks.'

A heavy silence fell in the room and Hannah felt like an intruder in the middle of her parents' pain.

'Can I see the photos?' Janie asked and reached for them. Her father quickly placed his hand over hers to stop her.

'Are you sure you want to?' he asked, but Janie wriggled her hand away and made a grab for the closest picture. Picking it up, she stifled a gasp and reached for another. Her eyes shone with tears as she went through the pile and then sadly pushed them toward Hannah.

'I never meant to hurt you both.'

Hannah barely heard her father's sad words as she flipped through photo after photo of a couple obviously in love, and she disloyally wondered what would have happened if he'd chosen the older sister in the first place.

Kevin picked up a bundle of letters held together by a red ribbon and frowned. 'I don't remember there being as many of these. Betsy must have added more later.' He untied them and looked at the envelopes. 'They're all to you.' He gestured towards Janie.

'To me?'

He nodded and handed them to her.

Hannah watched her mother open the first one and skim through the letter she took out. For the next few minutes she opened every envelope and did the same. Finally she glanced up again, and Hannah saw a different kind of pain in her eyes.

'She wrote the last ones about five years ago but never sent them, probably because I'd returned several earlier on and refused all her phone calls. They're full of apologies and her . . . love for me.' Janie's voice broke and slow, silent tears trailed down her cheeks. 'I wish she'd posted them.'

'Would you have replied?' Hannah asked.

'I don't know, but I like to think I would have.' She turned towards her husband. 'Thank you.'

'What for?' He sounded incredulous.

'Letting me love her again. I only wish it wasn't too late to tell her so.'

Kevin reached out to take hold of her hand. 'It's never too late. We can visit her grave — together, if you like.'

Janie nodded and touched his cheek. 'I'm going to see Jake.' Hannah jumped up but neither of them took any notice. No one ever knew how much time they had, and regrets were the worst thing to live with. She would give Jake another chance.

23

Jake stopped, bread knife in hand, at the sound of his doorbell ringing. He was in the middle of fixing a sandwich for his much-delayed lunch and wasn't in the mood for company after the morning he'd had. Setting down the knife, he wandered out to see who was disturbing him now.

'Hannah! What are you doing here?' he blurted out, and the hesitant smile left her face. 'Sorry. Didn't mean it that way. I'm just surprised to see you.'

'I expect you are. I was a bit short with you earlier.' A hint of colour warmed her cheeks as she stumbled over her words.

'You had good reason. How are things?'

'Strange.' Hannah gave him a wry smile.

'You coming in?' He didn't know

what else to say. 'How about a sandwich? I was just making one.'

'A sandwich?' she asked, as if he'd suggested they rob a bank. 'I didn't come over to be fed.'

'Okay.' Jake hated it when women expected men to read their minds. Usually he failed and they got angry.

'I want to talk,' Hannah declared and his heart sank. 'Don't look so petrified. I'm not going to bite.'

No, but you'll ask me things I can't answer and we'll be back at square one.

'Do you at least want to sit down?' he said. Even that seemed to perplex her, judging by the way she frowned, but finally she walked over to the sofa. Jake chose to sit in his usual chair, facing Hannah but not close enough to touch her. That seemed wise, since he wasn't sure of her mood. 'So, what's on your mind?' he asked her.

'You.' She blushed and Jake did too, his cheeks heating up as he wondered how much to read into her words. Before he could think of a suitable reply, she launched into a long, convoluted story about her parents and the unexpected contents of the box he'd dug up. He tried to follow the twists and turns her mind was making but gave up.

'You see, it's made me think. My mum has so many regrets about losing touch with Betsy, and my dad is worn down with the consequences of the choices he made.' Jake didn't see how this was connected to the two of them, but held his tongue. 'Most of their problems come from a lack of honesty. Things that should have been said but weren't.'

Jake got up and went to sit by her. 'Go ahead. Tell me what you came to say.'

A flash of uncertainty lit up her eyes. 'You won't laugh at me?'

'I'd never do that. *With* you sometimes, but never *at* you,' he promised with a smile, relieved when she managed to smile back.

She sucked in an audible breath, and

he found himself holding his own at the same time.

This was the craziest idea she'd had in a long time, Hannah thought, and for two pins she would run back next door to the safety of her cottage. But a picture leapt into her mind of her parents, and that gave her courage. She ploughed on before she could change her mind.

'It annoys me no end, but I'm attracted to you and need to find out if there's any way it could ever work between us. I don't think there is, but I'll always regret not trying if I . . . '

Jake leaned closer and stopped her rambling with a soft kiss. His firm, warm hands cupped her face, and she couldn't look anywhere but into his sparkling ice-blue eyes. 'You're braver than me, sweetheart.'

She pulled away slightly and fixed him with a hard stare. 'You mean you would have given up and said nothing?' She couldn't believe that — or maybe she just didn't want to.

'It's what I've been struggling to do. For your own good.'

'I hate it when people say that. I'll decide what my 'own good' is, thank you very much.'

His face lit up with a wide grin. 'That's more like my girl.'

'Is that what I am?' Hannah asked, her heart thumping in her chest. A shadow clouded Jake's eyes and she swallowed hard.

'There's a lot you don't know about me. I'd have thought you'd be more cautious.'

'You're doing a good job of talking me out of liking you,' Hannah retorted.

'It's probably for the best, even if you don't want to believe it right now.' Under his tan, Jake paled, and the small hint of uncertainty gave Hannah hope.

'Tell me what there is to know and let me decide for myself. At least give me that much,' she challenged, and waited.

Jake met Hannah's gaze straight on. The temptation to open up was overwhelming, but he couldn't rid himself of the idea that this woman, who'd been through so much already, deserved better than him. He remained silent.

'So that's it?' Hannah whispered, and stood up. He could hardly bear to look at her and acknowledge that he'd caused the distress written all over her face. 'I'm not sorry I came over. I thought you were made of stronger stuff than this, but you've proved me wrong again.'

He bit his tongue to hold back the words he ached to say. She walked over to the door as he watched her, rested her hand on the knob, and gave him one last lingering glance before leaving. As the door clicked shut behind her, he let his head slump into his hands. Waves of anger and frustration swept over him. She'd all but called him a coward, which riled him no end. He was a lot of things, but that wasn't one of them. Before he could talk himself out of it, Jake jumped up and rushed out of the house, calling out Hannah's name as he ran down the path after her.

Just as she turned to go through her own gate, he reached her and grabbed her arm. 'If you want the truth, you shall have it. It's not pretty, but you've asked for it.'

A small, triumphant smile tugged at her lips. 'I walked as slowly as I could.'

'You knew I'd follow?'

'Maybe not *know* exactly, but I hoped I hadn't read you completely wrong.' The laughing tease in her voice relaxed something inside Jake, and he grinned right back at her. Hannah took hold of his hand. 'Come on.' She led him towards his house again without saying another word. 'I think we need a cup of coffee before we start.'

He chuckled. 'You can have your coffee too, sweetheart, but I'm pretty darn sure we need something else first.' Jake drew her into his arms for a long, sweet kiss. With her soft, warm body cradled against his, nothing seemed as bad anymore. Things could still blow apart after they talked, but there was also hope, and he hadn't had that for a very long time.

Ten minutes later, they had their coffees and were sitting together at the kitchen table. Jake knew he mustn't put off his explanation any longer.

'Mikkel Christiansson is my stepfather and I've worked for him since college.'

'Willingly?'

How did she nail it so easily? 'Yes, and no.' He'd promised her honesty and had to follow through. 'He married my mother after my father died, but we've never really got on.' An understatement if ever there was one, but he didn't want to sound bitter.

'Did you have a good childhood before that?'

'Yeah. The best.' Jake smiled. Sometimes that got forgotten, and although it hurt, it was good to remember. The words tumbled out as he tried to convey what a wonderful man his father had been. Paul Erikson had been from Nashville, but had a Danish mother so had holidayed there a lot as a child and spent time studying in Copenhagen as part of his business degree. 'He started up an import/export business dealing in teak furniture. During the school year we lived in Nashville, and then spent our summers in the family's cottage on the island of Bornholm.'

'You loved it there,' Hannah said quietly. 'I can tell.'

Jake made an effort to describe the island that was so close to his heart. 'One day I'll take you there.' The promise hung in the air between them and Hannah nodded, giving him the sweetest smile.

'Was Mikkel unkind to you?'

He hesitated before answering, wanting to be fair. 'He loves my mother in his own way. Me, he has to tolerate for her sake. Money is his answer to everything, and she needed that security. My father's business wasn't doing well, and he left her with nothing.'

'Surely you could leave the property business now if you wanted to?'

'I got into some . . . difficulties as a young man, and Mikkel helped me out.'

'Is he blackmailing you?' The horror in Hannah's voice took Jake aback.

'I wouldn't quite put it that way.'

'Why not?' she persisted.

Nothing with this woman was easy, but Jake had promised himself to hold nothing back. He prepared to say the one thing that could drive her away.

24

'A man died, and I was blamed.'

The words, torn from Jake's throat, sliced through Hannah, and for a moment she couldn't speak. Of all the things she might have expected him to admit, that wasn't on the list. 'Was it your fault?'

He shook his head and stared down at the table. 'I didn't think so.' Then he glanced back up and frowned. 'Why do you believe me?'

Hannah reached out and took hold of his large hands. 'Because I trust you.'

'Why?' He shook his head. 'I've done nothing to deserve your trust, and you've been — '

'Shush.' Hannah rested a finger on his mouth to stop him saying any more. 'Don't compare yourself to Carlton Fenway, if that's what you were intending. He was bad to the core, but I've never thought that of you.' She couldn't resist smiling. 'Even when you tried to convince me you were nothing more than a flirtatious gardener, as opposed to a well-educated international businessman who reads heavy books on economics, computer programming and Aristotle in the original Greek in his spare time.'

'And how would you know about my reading habits, Hannah Green?' The sparkle returned to his eyes and he leaned in closer. 'Someone's been spying on me.'

'Certainly not!' she argued, but he held her gaze and she gave a small shrug. 'Well, maybe a little.' She blushed as she explained about her undercover detective work the morning after they'd met. They both laughed, but stopped at the same time, remembering what they'd been talking about before getting distracted. 'Sorry.'

'Don't be,' he reassured her, and pressed a light kiss on her forehead.

'Go ahead, then. You've done the hard part by telling me.' Hannah's heart raced, and she wished she was as sure as she'd hopefully made herself sound.

'I was sent to check on an abandoned warehouse outside Copenhagen as part of a development project my stepfather was considering. I found a man's dead body on the floor, but before I could do anything the police arrived and naturally they arrested me. Aaron Montego was a Cuban business acquaintance of my stepfather's.'

'Are you saying he had something to do with this man's death?'

Jake hesitated and she fought the urge to tell him to get on with it. 'I honestly don't know. My judgement might be coloured by my dislike of Mikkel. He's not always ethical in his business dealings, but it's a long way from that to murder.'

Hannah rested a hand against his cheek and he relaxed into her touch. 'You need to know, don't you?'

'Yeah, I do. My stepfather used his connections with the Danish police to get the case dropped, and I didn't ask too many questions because I was frightened. My mother didn't handle it well, and impressed on me how grateful we must both be to him.' His features tightened and waves of resentment emanated from him. 'Mikkel has always implied he did it for my mother's sake, not because he believed in my innocence.'

'I've been imagining all sorts of things, you know.'

'And this is better?' he said with obvious disbelief. 'You're crazy.'

'Since I believe you didn't do anything wrong, it's better than you having three ex-wives and a horde of children you're evading paying maintenance for,' Hannah declared, relieved when Jake burst out laughing. 'We'll have to confront your stepfather and get to the bottom of this.'

'We will?'

A sudden wariness trickled through her. Had she gone too far, too fast? For all she knew, Jake might not appreciate

244

her interference.

'Are you free for lunch on Sunday?' Jake's eyes gleamed and he seized her hands. 'Mikkel's always telling me to bring a guest, but I never do because of how things are. My mother will be there too. It's perfect.' He pulled her into a tight, warm hug. 'You meant it, didn't you?'

Hannah pushed away her uncertainty and nodded, giving him a broad smile and a kiss. *No regrets.* She was tired of playing it safe.

Jake hated to break the moment, but one thing hadn't changed between them and it was better to get it out in the open. 'You know I still have to work on the local development, don't you?'

The hint of a smile pulled at her lips. 'And you know I'll still be against it, don't you?' she teased.

Jake stroked his fingers all the way down her neck, resting against her throbbing pulse. 'May the best man . . . or woman win.' He pressed soft kisses along the trail his fingers had made and loved the way she shivered with pleasure. 'How about we discuss tactics over dinner tonight?'

'I can't.' Hannah sighed. 'There's my mum and dad to consider.'

He could've kicked himself for forgetting. 'Sorry. I just want to keep you here. I'm selfish.'

She wrapped her hands up around his neck and gave him a big kiss. 'No. Selfish is something you're definitely not. If you were you'd have thrown in the towel with your stepfather a long time ago.'

A rush of embarrassment crept up his neck and flooded his face. 'You'd better go before Jake the Rake returns to his renegade ways,' he joked, but she didn't smile.

'He's not real. Remember that. The real you isn't that way or I wouldn't be here now.' She rested her head in the curve of his shoulder and he wanted nothing more than to keep her there forever.

'Call me tomorrow, sweetheart. I'm sure we can make this work.' He spoke the words as much to reassure himself as her. He'd never made things work long-term with any woman before and was afraid he didn't know how.

'I'm sure, too,' Hannah said with a touch of the strength he'd admired in her from the very first day. 'Behave yourself.' She kissed him and let go before he could try to detain her any longer.

Jake smiled as he watched her leave, but it faded away as he remembered he had work to do. He'd considered asking Hannah what she knew about Andy Wareham before realizing that would be a stupid move. The man was her friend, whether Jake liked it or not, and he couldn't ask her underhand questions.

He went up to his bedroom and settled down with his laptop. It didn't take long. Nothing did these days if you knew how to look. He stared at the screen and wondered if Hannah knew about this. If he used the information in front of him, it could get the man on their side against his will, but what

247

would the woman he loved think of him then?

He printed off the information he needed and decided to make the phone call now and get it over with. A few minutes later he ran downstairs and headed back outside. Wareham happened to be working in the area and was about to take a late lunch break. They'd arranged to meet in the pub for a drink to talk about the resort development. Jake suspected it would turn out to be anything but friendly.

For late October, it was a decent day, and Jake enjoyed his walk down to the village. The harbour looked its best in today's sunshine and he stopped for a few moments by the beach to watch the waves crashing in over the sand. Maybe next summer he'd take up surfing. A knot formed in the base of his stomach as he wondered where he'd even be then. He and Hannah might be inching towards something together, but there was a lot they hadn't talked about yet. He sighed and headed for the pub, guessing before he got there what his reception would be.

He was spot on. Roscoe's polite enquiry as to what he wanted to drink was forced, and the locals propped up along the bar barely acknowledged him. Jake retreated to one of the corner tables and waited.

'Afternoon.' Andy Wareham appeared and Jake stood up to shake his hand. The other man ignored it and pulled out a chair to sit down. 'What did you want to see me for?'

Jake took a swallow of his beer and wondered how to play this. 'I want to better understand your objections to the planned development by my company.' That wasn't a bad place to start.

Andy launched into a detailed explanation which didn't tell Jake anything new, then fixed him with a hard stare. 'But you knew all that already, so why am I really here?' His sharp comment caught Jake unawares.

'It's part of my job to look into the background of the people speaking out against the resort. Sometimes they have motives they'd prefer to keep quiet that might help us in our bid if they become known.'

Andy's eyes narrowed. 'What exactly are you getting at, mate?'

'For example, let's say someone's wealthy wife is the daughter of the main rival to my company. It might benefit them for this scheme to be turned down so they could then build their own similar resort nearby.'

Andy slammed his glass down, sloshing beer out all over the table. 'You low-down, lying — '

'So you aren't married to Agnetha Pedersen?' Jake kept his voice low and the colour rose in Wareham's face.

'Yes, but we've kept it to ourselves,' Wareham muttered.

'Why?' Jake persisted.

'If Agnetha marries before she's thirty without her father's permission, she gets cut out of his will. And he's hardly likely to approve of her marrying me.' Disgust ran through his voice. 'We've only got another six months to keep quiet.' He looked beseechingly at Jake. 'It's not that we want the money, but it's complicated.' He shifted awkwardly in his seat. 'I shouldn't tell you this, but Gustav Pedersen isn't Agnetha's biological father. They never talk about it, but it's true all the same.'

Jake didn't ask any more. It wasn't his business, and he already had more than enough to satisfy his stepfather. 'I'm gonna have to pass this on to my boss.' He needed to be honest. 'Sorry.'

Andy glared. 'My marriage has absolutely nothing to do with my opposition to your scheme.' He pushed the chair back and stood up. 'I hope you can sleep at night.' Before Jake could reply he stalked out of the pub, making everyone turn and stare.

Jake knew that if he didn't tell Hannah about this meeting before Andy did, he'd be in deep trouble.

25

Hannah hung up the phone and counted to ten. It'd taken all her strength not to yell at Andy. Why hadn't he told her who he was married to? He'd expected her to be cross about Jake's interference last night, but in reality it was her old friend she was annoyed with. It hadn't occurred to him how bad it could look if this got out — and it would, because it was Jake's business to do whatever it took to get the planning application through. If that meant exposing one of the leading resort opponents who possibly had a vested interest in stopping the development, then he'd do so. Hannah noticed she had three messages on her phone and all were from Jake. No doubt the idiot thought she'd be mad at him.

As soon as she rang, he picked up, and she silenced him before he could speak. 'Be quiet and listen. Yes, I knew Andy was married. No, I didn't know who he was married to. I've told him he's an idiot and needs to make the news public before you do. Anything else you want to say?'

'I wouldn't dare.' Jake chuckled and she laughed along with him. 'Sorry for not trusting you to understand.'

Hannah was almost tempted to tease him a bit longer, but couldn't be so cruel. 'It's okay. We're both new at this. Do you want to come over?'

'Is it a parent-free zone now?'

She'd happily waved goodbye to her parents after breakfast, somewhat shocked to hear her mother offer her dad the spare room in her house until he sorted himself out. It was still hard to get her head around the fact that he was alive, and to forgive them both for deceiving her. Doing the wrong thing for the right reason wasn't something she found easy to rationalize.

'Are you still there?' Jake's worried question brought her attention back, and she apologised.

'Yes I'm here, and no they're not.' She hoped that made it plain.

'Good.'

She jerked her head back around to see Jake grinning at her from the kitchen doorway. 'I won't ask how you sneaked in.'

'I didn't *sneak* in,' he protested, with a broad smile all over his handsome face. 'I walked in barefoot, like a well-brought-up Danish boy. We never wear shoes in the house.'

'I'll remember that if I'm ever trying to hide anything from you.'

Jake crossed the room and Hannah knew she was in trouble — the good sort. She shrieked as he wrapped his arms around her and pulled her close. Before she could think of protesting, he began kissing her in a very determined way for several long, wonderful minutes.

'Right. Have we established there will be no hiding?' he teased, and started to tickle her ribs until she pleaded for mercy. 'I think I heard a yes. Should I tickle you again to make sure?'

'No, you beast.'

After a few more minutes he finally let go and flashed a very self-satisfied smile. 'Okay. First we're going on a walk, and then I'm taking you out to lunch.'

'A walk?'

'Yeah. You know, the thing people do when they place one foot in front of the other and move in a forward motion.'

How could a man be so annoying and fun at the same time? She'd never experienced this with any man before — the friendly back-and-forth between two people who appreciate each other's sense of humour. 'Okay, smarty. Where are we going to walk that's so important?'

A brief hint of uncertainty shadowed Jake's face, and she bit her tongue to stop from asking what was wrong. 'I want you to come with an open mind and let me give you an idea what this resort could be like and how it would fit into the village. After we finish, if you're still dead set against the plans, so be it.'

Hannah's tendency towards stubbornness reared its head and she longed to tell him to forget it.

He smiled and gave her another satisfying kiss. 'Thanks.'

'For what?'

'Not telling me to go and take a running jump.'

Being read so well was disconcerting and thrilling in equal parts. Hannah conceded by kissing him right back. 'Let's go before I change my mind.'

Jake wasn't sure when he'd started to see this proposed development in a new way. He thought it was when he'd really studied the details without Mikkel hovering over him. No matter what he thought of his stepfather, the plans were good. This could bring huge benefits to the village, and from what he could see, there would not be too many drawbacks.

He took hold of Hannah's hand as they walked along the road. They stopped just before starting down the hill and gazed out over the sea. The view from here was spectacular: rugged Cornwall at its best.

'What are your resorts like?' Hannah asked.

'We avoid popular tourist spots and always seek out beautiful, more remote places where guests can get a sense of peace outside of the resort. They're always on a relatively small scale, and are never built to a standard design, but to reflect their surroundings.' He sneaked a quick glance at her, but she didn't say a word. 'We hire as many staff from the local area as possible and base our menus around local products.'

A smile tugged at Hannah's mouth. 'I think it's unlikely you'll be feeding your health-conscious guests clotted cream and pasties.'

Jake tossed up his hands. 'You got me there. I was thinking more on the lines of all the wonderful fresh fish and vegetables y'all have around here.'

She wagged her finger at him. 'I'm

257

not conceding anything, so don't start to gloat, but I will admit it doesn't sound completely awful.'

For her that was a huge admission, and he chose his reply carefully, not wanting to sound patronising. 'Thank you. Hopefully now when you see the information our press people are starting to put out, you won't think it's a complete bunch of lies.'

Hannah gave him a thoughtful look. 'What are you going to do about Andy?'

'I gave him twenty-four hours to come clean.'

'After that?'

What did she think he was going to do? This was business, and while he still worked for Mikkel he'd do the job to the best of his ability.

'Stupid question?' Hannah said with a wry grin. 'Don't answer. I'd prefer not to know.'

Jake nodded. 'Now forget that and visualize where it would all go.' He pointed around them and gave her a general idea of where each building would be. 'We'd use Cornish stone in all the construction, and nothing would be any taller than the buildings here now.'

'But these houses would all be bull-dozed first, wouldn't they?' she probed. 'I know Rose Cottage isn't pretty, but it's mine now and I've grown fond of it. I'm sure other people feel the same way about their homes. Roscoe wasn't thrilled, was he?'

Jake turned defensive. 'He wanted to sell before I ever came, Hannah. You did too when you arrived. We've paid Roscoe enough that he can afford the new house he wants to buy. What's the problem?'

She raised up her hands and wrapped them around his neck, pulling him down so she could kiss him. Her light, feminine scent surrounded him and all he wanted was to kiss her back, so he did.

'There. That's better.' She let go with a triumphant smile. 'You know how much I hate to say you're right, don't you?' Her laugh trickled over his skin and he laughed along with her. She never ceased to surprise him; it was what kept him coming back over and over again. 'Right. I think we'll avoid the Green Dragon because of too many prying eyes. Instead you can treat me to fish and chips, and we'll eat them sitting on the wall overlooking the beach.'

'Works for me. I'm a pariah at the pub anyway,' he said with a casualness he didn't feel.

Hannah squeezed his hand. 'I'm sorry.'

'It's my own fault.' He shrugged. 'After this I'll be doing business my way or not at all. I'm tired of the underhand side of things.'

Her sea-green eyes shone. 'I don't think you want to do it anymore — honest or not. Am I wrong?' Before he could answer, she carried on. 'I'm taking a wild guess that you'd rather have a settled home. Maybe take up landscaping?'

This woman, who he'd only known a few short weeks, understood him inside and out. She wasn't afraid to say it like it was, either, which made him love her even more. *Not that I can tell her that yet. It's too soon for so many reasons.*

'Don't answer now. I don't need you to. Come on. I've got to get a couple of things in the shop first, and then we'll eat.'

He almost grumbled but caught her smile and simply agreed.

'You're learning,' Hannah teased, and slipped her hand back into his.

Jake started walking. It was a pleasure to be together, and he'd make the most of it. They soon reached the village, and he let her enter the shop first before ducking his head to avoid yet another low-level door.

Annie Rowse made a beeline in their direction as soon as she spotted them. Jake hung back, resting his hand lightly around Hannah's waist. 'Hannah, dear, you'm never going to believe what I just heard. Andy Wareham's married to some London girl who's mixed up with another one of those developers. They've been married a year and the boy never even told his own mother!'

Jake felt Hannah's body trembling

under his fingers and guessed she was trying not to laugh. She had a heck of a lot more restraint than he would.

'I won't bother buying any Hobnobs then, Mrs. Rowse,' Hannah said with a straight face. Jake didn't have a clue what she was talking about, but he'd get the full story later.

'They're sayin' he's dropping out of the protest group. Don't know if it's true.'

Uncharitable thoughts ran through Jake's head that the woman probably didn't care either, as long as she had something to gossip about.

'I wouldn't know. I must give him a ring to congratulate him,' Hannah said with her kindest smile.

'You'll be giving up yourself soon, I expect?' Annie Rowse's sharp eyes landed on Jake, and he gave her a full-on Jake the Rake grin, saying nothing.

'I don't have any plans to do so at present, but I promise you'll be the first to know,' Hannah replied. 'I need to pick up a few things now. See you again soon.' She hurried towards the nearest aisle and Jake followed along behind. He'd thought all women were slow shoppers, but in five minutes they were out of there and in the chip shop. Apart from placing her order, Hannah didn't speak again until they were sitting down outside and halfway through eating their lunch.

'Why didn't it occur to me?' Hannah mused.

Jake stopped with a chip halfway to his mouth. 'What are you getting at?'

'That people would think the same about us?'

He didn't know how to reply, so held his tongue until he could see where she was going with this.

'I've got to decide where my loyalties lie, don't I?' Hannah asked, and he heard the anguish in her voice. 'Aunty Betsy was a part of this community. I can't toss that to one side because of my . . . feelings for you.'

Jake couldn't believe what he was hearing.

'I need time to think about this,' she said very quietly, but with the determination he'd come to expect from her. She wrapped up the remains of her lunch and stood up, tossing the package in the nearby rubbish bin.

Jake wanted to say so much. *That's it? Goodbye, Jake?* Instead he simply nodded. 'Take all the time you need. If you don't know how I feel, I'll spell it out.' The words he hadn't planned to say anytime soon tumbled out. 'I love you.'

All the colour left Hannah's face and she swayed on her feet. 'I know you do.'

Jake refused to ask if she felt the same.

'I'll be in touch.' Her small voice sounded sad. 'One way or the other.' With that, she left him sitting alone. Again.

26

'The agenda for the strategic planning committee is out. The public meeting is scheduled for Friday morning at the city hall in Truro,' Andy explained, pushing a piece of paper across the kitchen table.

Mrs. Rowse had been wrong. Her friend didn't intend to back down, and had declared to anyone who would listen that his wife's family had nothing to do with his decision to oppose the scheme. Hannah was grateful to him for not asking her any personal questions. He'd surely heard about her disagreement with Jake, because it had been all around the village the next day. She guessed that piece of gossip was down to Matt Penlee, who'd been sitting next to them on the sea wall, and who just happened to be Mrs. Rowse's nephew.

'Isn't that quick? The three weeks for

objections will only just be up,' Hannah said.

'I did hear Christiansson put pressure on some of the councillors to move things along.' Andy shrugged. 'Nothing we can do about it. The good thing is, because so many people sent in objections, we get two speakers from our side. Three minutes apiece. I wish you'd reconsider,' he urged her.

No way could she stand up and speak against Jake. It'd broken her heart to leave him, and her doubts grew larger every day about whether she'd made the right decision. 'I can't, Andy. Don't ask me again, please.'

'I'm thinking about asking Mrs. Rowse.' He smiled and hurried on. 'I know she's a bit of a pain, but if they hear a shop-keeper speaking out against the scheme, I think it'll carry some weight.'

Hannah kept her doubts to herself. She wasn't sure they'd win. Jake had mounted a subtle publicity campaign, and one by one more people seemed to be changing their minds. Even the name they'd given the resort had struck a chord with the locals. Choosing to call it Senara's Refuge after the local saint associated with the village had been a smart move. It had got around that there would be at least fifty year-round jobs, a huge boost in a place where so much of the work was seasonal and young people often left the county to find employment.

'I'm sure she'll be very enthusiastic,' Hannah agreed.

Andy gave her a sideways look. 'What's up? You're not happy.' He picked up his coffee mug and took a swallow. 'It's none of my business, but . . . '

'You're right, it isn't,' she snapped. 'You didn't tell me about Agnetha. I'm not talking about Jake.'

'Fair enough. You know where I am if you change your mind,' he replied in his usual easygoing manner as he packed away the papers he'd brought. 'You will be at the meeting, won't you?'

Hannah's stomach churned but she nodded. 'Of course.' She stood up, wanting him to go.

'I'll be off. I'll see you next Friday if not before.' He didn't wait for her to say any more, and left.

She stood, staring out of the kitchen window and across to Jake's house, feeling nothing but a deep, aching need to be with him again.

★　★　★

Jake picked up his mobile for what must be the fiftieth time and slammed it right back down on the table. *Take all the time you need.* What a dumb thing to have said. He'd thrown himself into his work, but it didn't stop him thinking about Hannah constantly. The development campaign was going well; and with the momentum they had, things were looking up. He'd taken on more gardening jobs too, including one to redesign the garden belonging to one of the biggest houses in the area. Landscaping instead of just digging, just as Hannah predicted he wanted to do.

He should be worn out, but he wasn't sleeping either, spending far too many hours out on his patio in the cold, dark nights until even he was frozen to the bone.

The phone started to buzz, and he glanced at the display. His heart thudded.

'What time are you picking me up on Sunday?'

'Sunday?' He only managed to stumble out the single word, unable to believe how normal Hannah sounded.

'Lunch. Your parents. Had you forgotten?'

Forgotten? Did the woman have ice in her veins? 'Why are you doing this to me, sweetheart?' Jake whispered.

'Doing what? Sneaking up on you?'

Jake swung around to face Hannah, who was standing in the doorway with a bashful expression on her face. God, she was lovelier than he remembered, something he wouldn't have thought possible. 'Yeah. It's not good for my heart.'

'I supposed at your advanced age you have to be careful,' she teased, her cheeks flushing a bright shade of pink. 'How old are you, anyway? There's so much I don't know about you.'

Jake hurried over to stand in front of her and slid his hands around her waist. 'I'll be thirty-four in August. Ask anything else you like. I never want to hide anything from you again.'

She nibbled at her lip and it took all his self-control not to kiss her.

'Did you mean what you said the last time we spoke?'

'What was that?' he asked with as much innocence as he could muster. Judging by the way her face darkened and his hands were pushed away, he guessed she hadn't fallen for it.

'You know exactly what I mean, but if you insist I'll spell it out,' she hissed, and waited a second. When he didn't speak up, she gave a long drawn-out sigh and glared at him. 'You said you loved me. Did you mean it?'

Reaching out, he rested his hand

against her cheek, stroking his fingers over her velvety soft skin. 'Didn't I promise to always be truthful to you?' She nodded and a single tear made a long, slow path down her face. Jake wiped it away. 'There's your answer, then.'

'Aren't you going to ask me?' Hannah pleaded.

He shook his head. 'Nope.' It was killing him, but he needed her to offer it freely with no coercion on his part.

'Okay. This will make you gloat I'm sure, but yes I love you.'

Jake swept her back into his arms and clung onto her, burying his face in her glorious hair that tonight was lying loose around her shoulders. 'I'm not gloating, honey. I'm simply happy.'

'But I still — '

A long, slow kiss did the trick and silenced her; he'd known it would. She gave the sweetest of sighs and melted into him. 'Don't worry about that now,' he murmured. 'It's not important. This is.' He indulged them in another kiss and she didn't object. 'Thank you.'

'What for?' Hannah asked, fixing her beautiful sea-green eyes on him so that it took all his concentration to keep talking.

'Not letting me suffer any longer. I know I said take all the time you wanted, but I couldn't have hacked it much longer.'

She kissed him this time. 'Me too. I wouldn't be here otherwise.'

Jake eased away so he could better see her face. 'But what about the reason you left in the first place?' He couldn't go through this again.

'I was wrong to mix the two things up.' He squelched a grin, but she poked him in the ribs anyway. 'Don't gloat about this, either.'

'I wouldn't dare, love of my life,' Jake teased. 'And before you say any more, I know we've got a lot to sort out, but let's enjoy today first.' He cuddled her again, and she didn't object; far from it. Hannah's head rested against his shoulder and he wondered how he'd ever survived without her. She looked up at him and fluttered her eyelashes. It was such an un-Hannah-like gesture that he couldn't help laughing. 'What do you want now?'

'Want? Why would I want anything?'

Jake tightened his hold on her waist and leaned down to whisper in her ear. 'Because you're being girly and devious and you're usually neither of those things.'

'Will you come clothes shopping with me?' she wheedled, and he let out a load groan.

'Can't I dig up your garden, paint your house, or do your ironing for you instead?'

'Ironing? You must hate shopping.' Hannah giggled. 'Anyway, it's mainly your fault I need to go.'

For the life of him Jake couldn't follow her thought process.

'You want me to meet your parents tomorrow, and presumably impress them over lunch. I didn't bring any of my smart clothes with me from London. Therefore I need to buy something new.'

The pronouncement didn't allow any room for argument. 'We'll find out more about each other's tastes. Look at it as an opportunity to spend quality time together.'

Jake could think of far more pleasurable ways, but wasn't stupid enough to say so out loud. Hannah declared she would be kind and not drag him all the way to Plymouth, despite the shops being far better there. Her idea of giving him a break was apparently to only drive as far as Truro, about half an hour away. The shops there would hopefully offer enough selection without sending him over the edge.

'Let me get changed and we'll go.' He managed what he hoped was an agreeable smile and was rewarded with a big kiss.

Four hours later he was amazed to find he'd been talked into getting a haircut. *Just a trim, Jake dear*. A smart blue shirt and grey trousers were added to the shopping, along with a soft black leather jacket. As soon as Hannah told

274

him he looked hot in it, he'd been dazzled enough to buy the thing. The fact that he rarely wore a coat was obviously irrelevant — clearly he'd be wearing one tomorrow.

Hannah had managed this after modelling endless dresses for him that all looked wonderful on her. Jake almost said at one point that she'd be beautiful wearing a paper bag, but stopped himself at the last second. To save himself any more torture, he'd zeroed in on a simple linen sleeveless dress that showed off her figure without being revealing. He commented that it was a pretty colour of green, and was informed the shade was called peppermint and very fashionable. Jake guessed his mother would approve.

When he asked for the bill, Hannah tried to argue, but he got one over on her for once by declaring that if it was his fault she needed a new dress, then he should be the one to pay for it. She couldn't easily dispute that and gave in almost graciously.

'I think we're done,' she said. 'I have some shoes that'll go with this.'

Jake gave thanks for small mercies. 'Right, let's go.'

'Home.' Hannah took hold of his hand, and all Jake could think was how wonderful that sounded. They'd face his family together and hopefully give him the chance to begin again.

27

'*Velkommen*, welcome to our home,' Mikkel Christiansson greeted them out on the doorstep, and Hannah stiffened her posture under the man's intense scrutiny. He stood to one side to let an elegant blonde woman step out past him.

'My dear. You must be Hannah. We are so happy to have you join us today.' Her bright blue eyes rested on Jake. 'Janik. Aren't you looking smart today. Very nice leather jacket.' The mischievous smile she gave Hannah said she guessed who deserved the credit.

'You too, *Mør*.' He leaned forward to kiss his mother, and Hannah was struck by the resemblance between the two. Out of the corner of her eye she noticed Mikkel's face darken as his unsmiling gaze rested on Jake.

'Let us go inside. Elsa has a

wonderful meal ready for us,' Mikkel declared, sliding his arm around his wife's shoulder and pulling her closer to him.

'I do not want Hannah to think I did it myself.' She blushed. 'I have an excellent cook. Janik says you have never been to Denmark, so we are having a traditional *koldt bord*, or cold buffet. They way you can sample many different things.'

'I'm looking forward to it very much,' Hannah said, genuinely keen to try the foods she knew Jake loved and missed.

'Elsa always brings treats for us from London. The Cornish do not appreciate Danish-style pickled herrings, so I am told.' Mikkel laughed, and the warm sound took Hannah by surprise.

They all went inside and settled in a charming sunroom overlooking the garden. 'Please excuse me. I will go and see if Petra has our meal ready,' Elsa explained, and left the three of them alone.

Jake began, 'There's something I

want to talk about while — '

'Show some manners, *søn*,' Mikkel cut him off. 'We should offer our guest a drink.'

'Of course. I apologize.' The icy tone in Jake's voice sent a shiver running through Hannah's blood.

'Elsa always has a glass of champagne before lunch. Would you care to join her?' Mikkel asked while opening the bottle he had ready in an ice bucket on the sideboard.

Hannah thanked him and accepted, even though she'd have preferred water to keep her head clear. Jake took a bottle of beer from his stepfather without a word. As Elsa came back into the room, Mikkel immediately poured her a glass, his face softening as he rested his gaze on her. '*Skal*.' He raised his beer bottle.

Hannah followed his lead, as everyone made eye contact with each other in what Jake had already told her was the Danish traditional way before taking a drink.

A buzzing sound interrupted them and Mikkel pulled his phone from his pocket, frowning at the screen. 'I am sorry, but this is important. Please excuse me for a moment.'

'Let us sit down.' Elsa gestured towards the two large sofas and they all made themselves comfortable.

Jake held on to Hannah's hand and sucked in a breath. '*Mør*, there's something I want to talk to you about.'

Elsa's eyes twinkled as she glanced between the two of them. 'You have some good news maybe?'

A hot rush of embarrassment flamed Hannah's face as she realized what the other woman was getting at.

'No.' Jake flashed her a quick grin. 'Not yet, anyway.' The humour left his face and he glanced over at the door. 'There are two things I need to know about, and Mikkel refuses to discuss either. He instructed me before not to talk to you about them, but — '

'I have known this for a while, Janik, and have been a coward. It was easier not to do anything about it. No one got hurt that way.'

Was the woman blind?

'I've been hurting for a long time,' Jake whispered. The brief flash of pain dimming his mother's eyes almost made him wish he'd kept quiet, but one glance at Hannah and he knew he had to do this for both their sakes. 'I believe Mikkel knows things about Aaron Montego's death that he's keeping from me.'

'I hope you're not accusing him of murder?' Horror filled Elsa's voice.

'No,' Jake conceded. He had no proof of anything. 'But I do suspect he knows more than he's admitting.'

'Do you indeed?' Mikkel's steely words cut into the conversation. He stood in the doorway, glaring at them all. 'Is this why you brought Miss Green for lunch — because you didn't have the nerve to face me alone?'

'Mikkel! What a way to talk in front of our guest,' Elsa remonstrated, and he had the grace to look ashamed.

We'll have to tackle your stepfather and get to the bottom of this.

Jake took hold of Hannah's hand and her sympathetic smile gave him courage. 'Hannah understands it's important for me to know the truth and wanted to be with me today. It's not a question of nerve. It's caring.' *Read into that whatever you like.*

'What about lunch?' his mother asked.

'Lunch can wait.' Mikkel's snapped-out reply made Elsa blanch, and it took all Jake's control to bite back his anger. 'You were found with Montego's blood on your hands. What was I supposed to think? My main concern was to protect your mother at all costs.'

'I was innocent, and you did nothing to help me prove that. Paying off the police doesn't count.'

His stepfather's face took on the appearance of granite. 'How dare you. I used certain connections of mine to plead your case, and maybe if I hadn't you'd be in jail now. I did not bribe anyone, and I never have done despite your low

282

opinion of my morals.'

For the first time Jake wondered if he'd been too quick to misjudge Mikkel. He was a plain-spoken man, born on the rough edges of Copenhagen, and had made himself a success through his own hard work. Plus, his love for Elsa was obvious for everyone to see.

'So do you know who did kill Montego?'

Mikkel walked over to the sideboard, grabbed a bottle of beer, opened it and took a long swallow before speaking again. 'I do not know who pulled the trigger. I am sure Lars Pedersen was behind the killing, but despite ten years of searching I still have no proof. It broke your mother's heart, and I have done everything I could to prove your innocence. You dare to stand there and accuse me of not telling you the truth, but the truth is that I said nothing because I did not want your thanks when all I had done was fail.'

Jake was speechless, and only the reassuring touch of Hannah's hand on his arm enabled him to keep it together. 'But why would Pedersen do that to me? I barely even know the man.' It didn't make sense. An odd look passed between his parents, and Jake's heart sank as he wondered what was coming next.

'You don't have to explain, Elsa,' Mikkel murmured, but she shook her head.

'Yes, I do. Janik deserves to know. It has been a secret for too long.' She smoothed down her skirt and turned to face him with a tiny, brave smile. 'Your father was married before me to Bergitte Pedersen. They were very young, just out of school, and had a daughter together.'

'Agnetha is my half-sister?' Jake asked, unable to believe what he was hearing.

His mother nodded, wiping away a tear. 'Unfortunately, the marriage did not last. Bergitte got remarried to Lars Pedersen, but he was always resentful of Paul for the fact that he was her first husband and the father of her daughter.

That he and Bergitte were unable to have children themselves did not help. Eventually she left him because of his insecurity, and his dislike of this family became more irrational.'

Mikkel patted Elsa's hand. 'None of this was your fault.' He faced Jake. 'Lars and I grew up in the same neighbourhood and have been business rivals since I sold more bottles of Coke than he did at the local fair when we were ten.' He gave a wry smile. 'When I married your mother, he became more determined to best me. It is why he competes with me in the same business and why I am sure he saw hurting you as a way to get his idea of revenge.'

An odd sort of peace surrounded Jake. 'Thank you. Both of you.'

'You are not angry?'

Jake stood up and faced his stepfather. 'No. I can live with never knowing the whole truth. I'd prefer to of course, but I'm not going to spend my life fretting over it.' He swallowed hard. 'I hope you can accept my apology.'

Mikkel's face coloured and he shifted awkwardly from one foot to the other. 'I've been a stubborn idiot. You've done so much for me, and I've thrown most of it back in your face. I'm not looking to replace my father, but I hope we can at least be friends?' He held out his hand and waited. For a few seconds his stepfather didn't move a muscle, and Jake wondered if he was too late.

'That's all I've ever wanted, Janik.' Mikkel's quiet statement tightened the emotion in Jake's throat. 'I am not good at sharing my feelings. Your mother understands this.' He gave her a shy smile. 'Luckily she loves me anyway.'

Why had he never seen that before? Jake wondered. Money had little, if anything, to do with their marriage. His mother had always shown her love for Mikkel in her own way, as he had in his. She had fallen for a man from a very different background and accepted him as he was. Jake knew Hannah was now offering him that same unconditional love, and was beyond grateful.

'Friends,' Mikkel declared, and shook Jake's hand firmly. 'Right. Now maybe we can enjoy our lunch.'

'That's an excellent idea. I'm starving,' Hannah announced with a broad smile.

'Good,' Mikkel responded. 'We have enough food for an army, as you English say.' He offered her his arm and Hannah took it. With a big smile Jake did the same to his mother, and they walked towards the dining room. What a day this was turning out to be. Now he'd begin his self-appointed task to make Hannah fall in love with all things Danish, as she had with him. He couldn't remember being this happy and relaxed in a long time.

They all settled around the dining room table, and his mother brought out a dish of *marinerede sild*, the pickled herrings he loved.

'I think these must be an acquired taste,' Hannah whispered to him after she'd tried one, adding that she doubted they'd ever top her list of favourite foods.

Next there was a huge selection of

different dishes, from the wonderful *frikadeller* meatballs to *gravad laks*, delicious salt-cured salmon served with a dill and mustard sauce. The cook had included a large platter of smørrebrød, and Jake persuaded Hannah to try several of the open sandwiches for which Denmark was famous. The thin roast beef with *remoulade* and crispy onions on dark rye bread was her top pick and just happened to be Jake's favourite as well. For dessert they had a selection of fresh fruits and wonderful Danish cheeses, but Elsa also brought out a large bowl of the stewed strawberries with whipped cream they all loved. Jake couldn't resist trying to get Hannah to pronounce the name of the dish, *rødgrød med fløde*, and none of them could stop themselves from laughing, including Hannah.

'Okay. I'm pitiful,' she joked.

'I do believe Janik will have to give you Danish lessons,' Elsa declared, and she and Mikkel laughed at the obvious implication behind her words.

Jake blushed, and Hannah resembled a beetroot. 'I think it's time we were going,' he declared, and she looked so relieved he almost kissed her, but didn't want to embarrass her any more.

They made their escape while they still had some privacy intact. There was a lot to talk about, but it could wait. He'd put the poor woman through enough for one day.

28

Hannah watched out of her kitchen window, waiting for Jake to appear with their morning croissants. This was becoming a habit her hips might not thank her for soon.

As he came into view, she allowed herself a quiet smile. The smart clothes she'd got him into at the weekend were long abandoned, and he was back to his usual disreputable jeans and worn-out T-shirt. Still, he looked as good as ever to her.

'Good morning, beautiful,' he announced with a big smile as he strode in the back door and swept her into a tight hug. After giving her a kiss, he finally eased away. 'I'm not used to brooding, and I hate going on about this, but I can't get it out of my mind that I've got a half-sister I didn't know about. I wonder if *she* knows. Andy mentioned that she wasn't Pedersen's biological daughter, but he didn't say anything else, did he?'

Hannah shook her head. 'No, and I didn't ask because it wasn't any of my business. Just as a guess, I'd say she doesn't have a clue. If Andy had heard of the connection to you, I'm fairly sure he'd have mentioned it. She hasn't been living here; they've been meeting up on weekends in London where she still works. But maybe she'll be with him at the meeting tonight.'

An attempt at a smile tugged at Jake's mouth. 'Not an ideal place to have a private discussion.'

Hannah chose her reply carefully. 'I'm not sure it's your story to tell anyway.'

He gave her a long, hard stare. 'You're right, of course, even though I wish you weren't.'

Hannah fought against smirking. 'Find something to do and keep yourself busy.'

'Bossy woman,' he grouched, but gave her another kiss. 'I've come to work some more on your garden for a couple of hours, then I promised Mikkel we'd go over the game plan for tomorrow over lunch.'

'Before I tell you something I want you to know, my decision has nothing to do with us,' Hannah hurried to explain. 'If the plans are approved despite the objections, I'm not going to hold out any longer. I'll go ahead and sell.'

Jake frowned. 'Are you sure?' He instantly apologized as she glared at him. 'Of course you are. Sorry.'

Hannah sensed his hesitation, and it didn't take a genius to guess what was on his mind. 'Let's not rush anything else. I want to get to know you better and sort out what I want to do next before we make any plans.' His gentle smile told her she'd hit the right note. They'd both had their challenges, and the last thing she wanted was to have any more regrets. She hoped she wouldn't be that stupid again, no matter how much she loved Jake — and she did very much.

'Breakfast and then digging,' Jake declared, and picked up the white paper bag he'd dropped on the counter when he'd arrived. The sweet scent of warm chocolate filled the air and Hannah sighed.

'Oh, go on, talk me into it.'

'We could sit outside,' Jake suggested with a questioning smile.

'It's far too cold for me. You go ahead if you want. I'm staying here in the warm,' Hannah declared firmly, snatching the bag from his hands and pulled out a roll before he could take them away. She sank her teeth into the crisp, flaky pastry and groaned with pleasure. 'That's wonderful. I think I'll let you stay.'

'Aren't you generous. I'll fix our coffees if you're not going to,' Jake grumbled, and wandered over to the coffee pot.

Soon they were sitting at the kitchen table, but Hannah knew by how quiet he was, and she guessed from the way he'd stroke her hand occasionally without really looking at her that his mind was elsewhere.

'I'm going to clear out the rest of Betsy's papers while you work. Make sure you dig where I can keep an eye on you — that way I can ogle without having to crane my neck,' she teased.

'You're impossible,' Jake said, cracking a wide smile. 'I'm off.' He pushed the chair back and stood up. 'My shirt's staying on today, so you can look all you like.'

'Spoilsport,' Hannah shouted to his retreating back as he left in haste. At least she'd got him to smile again.

★ ★ ★

Jake wasn't sure how he'd got through the last twenty-four hours with so much on his mind. Once the meeting was finished, his job would be too. The new understanding between him and Mikkel had helped when they'd discussed his next plans. He'd be talking about things with Hannah, but she'd expect him to know his own mind, and he respected that because it was nothing more than he would assume from her too. Mikkel had tentatively raised the possibility of him managing the new resort, but Jake wasn't keen on the idea. He was considering doing a landscaping course as a good starting point and then go from there. Luckily, money wasn't really an issue, because he'd been well-paid for several years and wasn't an extravagant man, which Hannah would say was obvious from the state of his wardrobe and the beat-up truck he drove. But she'd say it with such a beautiful smile and kiss that he couldn't be offended.

He finished buttoning his crisp white shirt and tucked it into his suit trousers, then added his father's monogrammed cufflinks as the final touch before slipping on the coat. At least his recent haircut meant he didn't have the usual battle with his unruly curls. He checked his appearance in the mirror and decided it was as good as it would get. Much as he would've liked to drive to the meeting with Hannah, she'd suggested it would be better to travel separately and get together when the meeting was over.

The roads were busy, and by the time he reached Truro and parked he didn't have much left to spare. Once he tracked down the council chamber, he went in and glanced around. The room was packed, but he easily spotted Hannah's gleaming hair down in the front row. On the opposite side of the room were Mikkel and his mother, so he went to join them.

The general buzz of conversation went quiet as the strategic planning committee chairman stood up and brought the meeting to order. Once he had run through the rules, he announced the first application to be discussed, which was theirs. A planning officer gave an introduction.

The first speaker for the opposition was Andy Wareham, and Jake craned his neck to watch the man get up from his seat. He spotted a woman sitting next to him with curly blonde hair and wondered if it was Agnetha. Andy finished his three-minute presentation, and then it was Mrs. Rowse's turn.

They did well, but Jake didn't sense the huge swell of support they might have had a month ago before their publicity campaign. Next came the two speakers from the parish councils of Polzennor and the adjoining village, who got their three minutes each. Then Jake stood up and went forward to speak. He couldn't help glancing at Hannah, and was cheered by her encouraging smile. Once he was done, the last person scheduled to speak was Mikkel, who'd elected to use the second spot on behalf of the applicants himself. He rarely got so involved, but this project had become very personal for him.

A noise started in the back of the room and grew louder as several people stamped their feet on the wooden floor and began doing a slow hand-clap.

'Go back where you belong — leave our village alone!' one burly man yelled, and a policeman pushed his way through to grab hold of him and take him outside. Several others called out abuse at Mikkel, and Jake heard accusations of bribery and corruption. Mikkel's face turned to stone and he stopped speaking. More policeman came in, and there was chaos until they removed the half-dozen or so troublemakers. Jake didn't recognize any of them from the village and wondered if they'd been sent by Pedersen to disrupt the proceedings. He glanced back at his stepfather, who gave him a tight smile before carrying on with his presentation.

'What happens now?' Elsa whispered.

'The committee will discuss the application before they take a vote. Then they'll announce the result,' Jake explained.

There was the low hum of conversation as the audience waited, and finally the chairman stood back up. 'After a unanimous vote, the application is approved. We believe the Senara's Refuge Spa Resort will be a boost to the local area, and are sure the planners will work with the community to fit in as smoothly as possible.'

Apart from a couple of boos, there was a general sense of approval, and the meeting began to break up. Jake immediately headed across to Hannah, relieved to see she didn't look too disappointed.

'Hi, sweetheart.' He slid his arm around her waist and gave her a quick peck on the forehead.

Andy Wareham held out his hand and Jake let go of Hannah to shake it.

'Congratulations.'

'I hope you're not too disappointed?' Jake said.

Andy shrugged. 'Not really. I expected we'd lose. You had too much momentum going, and better publicity. I hope it works out well and doesn't destroy the area.'

'That was never our intention. It doesn't benefit us to be at odds with the local community.'

'Of course,' Andy said stiffly. 'Good night.'

The woman who'd been standing next to Andy turned to speak, but the smile left her face as she stared at Jake, who froze as his gaze took in her white-blonde hair and ice-blue eyes, the mirror image of his own. Vaguely he was aware of Hannah taking hold of his hand.

'Andy, aren't you going to introduce me to your friends?' The woman's crisp tone held clear hints of a Danish accent.

'I'm Janik Eriksen,' Jake jumped in before Andy could speak, automatically using his real name. He stuck out his hand, but out of the blue the woman seized hold of his wrist and peered at the cufflink fixed in his shirt sleeve.

'Where did you get that?' She pointed to the heavy engraved silver in the shape of Denmark, but with the island of Bornholm disproportionately large.

Before Jake could reply, Elsa spoke up from behind him. 'They belonged to your father, Paul Eriksen.' Her voice was quiet but firm.

'My father? But . . . ' The woman stared at Jake and her skin turned ashen. 'Oh, my God.'

29

'Eerie, isn't it?' Jake tried for a touch of humour, but her expression remained horrified. 'How about we go somewhere quiet to talk?'

'There's a small coffee shop just around the corner,' Hannah whispered, and Jake threw her a grateful smile. He glanced back at Agnetha and waited for her to say something. Anything.

'Good idea,' Andy spoke up instead, and took hold of his wife's arm. 'All right, dear?'

She managed to nod, and they all made their way out through the crowd. It took a few minutes because they kept having to stop and speak to people. Mikkel joined them, and Jake noticed a brief conversation going on between him and Elsa.

Nobody spoke again until they were in the coffee shop, ordered their drinks,

301

and found a large table over in a quiet corner.

'Do you want to explain what's going on?' Andy said with his arm wrapped protectively around his wife's shoulder.

Jake looked to his mother for guidance. He wasn't sure how much to say.

'How much do you know about your biological father, my dear?' Elsa asked.

Agnetha shrugged. 'Nothing. When I was little, my mother told me she was married before, and that Lars had adopted me when they got married. As I got older, I asked them both several times, but they would get upset — particularly Lars, so I stopped asking.'

'I see,' Elsa said sadly. With a sigh she started to tell the story, and as he had the first time, Jake sensed how much it cost her. When she finished, Mikkel squeezed her hand and then started to speak. He explained who he was, and about his antagonistic relationship with Lars Pedersen.

Agnetha's eyes widened as she listened. 'Goodness. I never could have imagined all that.' She focused hard on Jake again. 'All of a sudden I've acquired a half-brother. I don't know what to say.'

'You're not the only one. I only found out last weekend, so I'm still in shock too,' Jake replied with a lightness he didn't feel.

'It explains a lot. Lars was a good father to me in his own way, but he was very controlling. Still is.' She gave a shy smile at Andy. 'He's not happy about my marriage.'

'But you are?' Elsa asked, and now Agnetha broke into a wide grin.

'Oh, yes. I am moving here with Andy now.'

Andy turned to Jake. 'So your interfering did some good. Thank you.'

Jake hadn't expected to be thanked for doing something that hadn't been initiated with the best of intentions, but didn't argue. 'Hopefully we can get to know each other better.' He hesitated to say the words to his new sibling.

'I'd like that, *bror*.'

Jake blinked back tears as Agnetha called him 'brother' for the first time. 'Me too, *søster*,' he returned the compliment, and now tears filled her eyes.

'Paul would have been very proud of you both,' Elsa declared. 'Where does your mother live now, Agnetha?'

'She returned to her old home in Viborg on the Jutland Peninsula. Next month she will travel to visit us.'

'We would like you all to come and have lunch with us then,' Mikkel offered. Jake admired his stepfather because he knew how difficult it was for him to accept Elsa's past. He'd proved himself a better man than Lars Pedersen who, had let it twist him and cause untold trouble.

'Will you be staying here?' Andy asked Jake, and for a second he wasn't sure how to reply.

'He'd better be,' Hannah said with a warm laugh, and Jake wanted to kiss her in front of everyone but guessed it would embarrass her.

She couldn't believe she'd just said that. His eyes glowed as they rested on her, and all she craved was for them to be on their own.

'I do not want to be the first to leave, but I have work to do,' Mikkel interrupted, and Hannah wanted to hug him. 'I do believe I have a resort to build.' He chuckled. 'It was a pleasure to meet you, and we will see you again soon,' he addressed Andy and his wife. Then he stood and pulled out Elsa's chair for her to join him.

The four of them who were left sat quietly for a few moments, sipping their neglected drinks. 'What was your, uh, our father like?' Agnetha suddenly asked.

Jake pulled out his wallet, retrieved a photo, and passed it across the table. 'We look like him.' Hannah glanced over his shoulder and saw how right he was, because both had Paul Eriksen's white-blond curls and magnetic eyes.

'He was a lot of fun and very adventurous. He loved the outdoors, and we did a lot of hiking and sailing together.' Jake's voice cracked. 'I still miss him every day.'

'I'm sure you do. Is Mikkel a good man?' Agnetha asked, and he instantly nodded. The new closeness with his stepfather had brought Jake a level of peace he'd desperately needed.

'Yes, he is. He's not the charming, easygoing man our father was, but when you get to know him he's very decent and would do anything for the people he cares for.' He'd never verbalized that, before and Hannah longed to say how proud she was of him.

'You are lucky. I have told Lars I do not want his money. It comes with too many conditions, and I have all I need here.' Agnetha touched Andy's arm and his face coloured.

'When you come for lunch, we'll get my mother to bring out the old photo albums and videos,' Jake said, and then frowned. 'By the way, how did you recognize my cufflinks?'

Agnetha smiled and reached up to undo a fine silver chain hanging around her neck before pulling it out from under her blouse and lying it down on the table. Hannah saw that the silver pendant hanging from it was identical to Jake's cufflinks, and both sets were engraved with Paul Eriksen's initials. 'My mother gave me this when I turned eighteen. She'd had them made especially for their wedding — the cufflinks for him and this necklace for her. This was the only clue I ever had; she told me they were something of a joke, because he always talked about his home on the island of Bornholm.'

'She's right, he did,' Jake murmured, 'and we still have a home there. I'm glad I wore them today. I'd wondered if you would be here, but couldn't have said anything because it wasn't my story to tell.' He shot Hannah a smile. 'As this lovely lady informed me.'

Andy laughed. 'I think we all might

have guessed something was up, look-ing at the pair of you.'

'He's right, you know,' Hannah added. 'Anyway, it's all worked out, and thank goodness it's out in the open at last.' So many things were, and she was glad.

'Hear, hear,' Andy concurred. 'I think we need to leave you now. I expect Agnetha would like to ring her mother. There's a lot to be said, I'm sure.'

His wife didn't look very happy about the prospect, and Hannah sympathized. No doubt, as with Janie, this young woman had kept the peace by not asking her mother too many awkward questions. Hannah wanted to reassure her that in the end it would be for the best; that she was sure they, too, would find a new intimacy; but she held her tongue.

'There is indeed.' Agnetha pushed her chair back and stood up, and they all did the same. 'It has been quite a day.' She held her hand out to Jake. 'I am so glad we have met.'

He shook her hand and bent to kiss her cheek, then shook Andy's hand next. 'Take care of her.'

'Oh, I will,' Andy promised.

They left, and Hannah couldn't stifle a relieved sigh.

'Alone at last,' Jake whispered in her ear, and pulled her into a warm hug. 'I think it's time to go home.'

'Sounds wonderful.'

He glanced out of the window. 'The weather's still decent. How about I cook you the hamburgers I promised weeks ago for our lunch?'

'Great,' Hannah agreed, and bit her tongue on saying any more for now.

'But?' He'd sensed her hesitation, and she couldn't be more pleased.

'Oh, I want the hamburgers, but afterwards there's a lot we need to sort out.'

Jake's wry smile warmed her heart. 'Understatement, sweetheart. I suspect we've got enough to talk about to occupy more than a few hours.' He pulled her closer and whispered,

'Hopefully we'll sneak in a few kisses while we're putting our world to rights.'

'I don't think it's too bad right now, do you?' she teased.

'Nope, it sure isn't.' He grinned. 'Come on. I'm goin' to feed you, then you can talk me to death.'

'I hope not,' Hannah said with feeling. It would work out, because they'd make sure of it. But she still crossed her fingers behind his back, just to make sure.

30

'I'm stuffed.' Hannah groaned and pushed her chair away from the table before she could be tempted to eat any more. Jake had grilled the most wonderful hamburgers she'd ever eaten, so juicy and flavourful that she'd devoured hers in a matter of minutes.

Jake flashed the same charming, satisfied smile he'd first used on her all those weeks ago. Who would have thought they'd be here today ready to discuss a future together? Falling in love again had been the last thing on her mind when Hannah had arrived at Rose Cottage. A shiver of apprehension ran through her, but in a second Jake reached across the table and cradled her hand with his own.

'It's going to be fine. You haven't made another mistake. I promise I'll never let you down.' His quiet words seeped into her and she almost managed a smile.

'How can you be so sure?' She left unspoken what they both knew — that she'd believed herself to be in love before, trusted the man, and been hung out to dry when he betrayed her in so many ways she couldn't begin to count them.

'Come sit with me,' Jake urged, and shifted his chair back away from the table. Hannah slid over into his lap and snuggled into his neck, relishing his clean fresh scent, the one imprinted on her brain. 'I'm sure because of you, and because of me. We're not teenagers, honey. We've been around the block a few times, and life hasn't always been a breeze.'

'You can say that again,' Hannah said wryly. 'And no, please don't take me literally.'

His eyes glittered and he lowered his mouth to hers, sinking them into another tempting kiss. With his arms wrapped tightly around her, Hannah felt his racing heart beating against hers.

'I'm ready to put down roots, and you are too,' he asserted, and Hannah couldn't argue. 'You know I'm interested in landscaping, and I might still do some real estate deals on the side, just small-scale.' Jake went quiet for a few seconds and she waited. 'Mikkel offered me a job managing Senara's Refuge. I turned him down, but then I thought about it some more.'

Hannah frowned. 'I can't see you enjoying that somehow.'

'No, I wouldn't.' He fixed his gaze on her. 'But what about you?'

'Me! You must be mad.'

'Why?' Jake asked in genuine surprise. 'You're a smart woman. You're used to dealing with money, and people. You're almost local. I think you'd be ideal.'

She gaped at him. 'Come off it. Do you really think anyone would entrust running a business to a woman who barely avoided ending up in prison for financial wrongdoing?'

'Mikkel would,' Jake said quietly. 'He likes and respects you.'

So many arguments against the idea raced around Hannah's brain. Briefly, she let herself imagine how she'd feel about the possibility if things were different. She'd be exhilarated. It would be scary and a huge challenge, but one she'd relish. 'How can you possibly know that?'

Jake smirked. 'Because he said so when I asked him.'

'You what?' Hannah jerked out of his embrace and glared at him. 'How dare you. You had no right — '

'Yes, I did.' His calm reply stunned her into silence. 'I love you, and I want the best for you. I would hope you'd do the same for me.' He grasped hold of her shoulders. 'Wouldn't you help me out if you could?'

Put that way, he was right, and the hint of a grin pulling at his lips told Hannah that he knew exactly what she was thinking. 'Stop being so smug,' she said with a smirk. He burst out laughing and she couldn't help joining in. When they eventually quieted down, he took her back in his arms and kissed her forehead.

'We're goin' to have to work on you being able to take instead of just giving, sweetheart,' Jake whispered against her skin, and a rush of heat flamed her face. 'Let's start with this.' He shifted in the seat and fumbled in his jeans pocket. The next moment a small black leather box appeared in his hand, and Hannah's heart thumped in her chest. 'I could get down on one knee, but I much prefer having you on my lap, so we'll do this my way.'

Any idea of protesting died away, and she tried hard to remember to breathe.

'You're all I need, for always.'

Hannah suspected those were tears she saw making his eyes shine, and swallowed hard to stop from crying herself.

'I love you. Be my wife, and I'll cherish you every single day we're lucky enough to have together.'

His simple promise was all she needed. He flipped open the box to reveal a stunning square-cut diamond ring, and Hannah couldn't speak for several moments as she fought back tears. 'I love you so much. I don't know why we've been this lucky, but I'm not going to question it any longer. The answer is yes, yes, yes, a thousand times yes.'

'Heck. I hope you don't mean I need another nine hundred and ninety-nine rings!' Jake teased, and she mock-smacked his arm. 'Hey, behave yourself or I'll change my mind.' His raucous laughter filled the air, and she'd never such happiness on anyone's face before. The knowledge that he was happy because of her made Hannah's head swim.

'Too late. You asked. I said yes. Put the ring on my finger, and you'd better hope that I like it.'

Jake picked up her hand and slid the ring into place before giving her a satisfied smile. 'Happy now?'

She turned her hand to catch the light from different angles. With a straight face, she glanced back up at him. 'I suppose it'll do.'

'It'll do?' A wicked smile crept across his handsome face. 'Would you care to rephrase that and show a little more enthusiasm?'

'No. I do believe I'll stick with my original opinion.'

Jake nodded and stood up, sliding her off his lap but scooping her up into his arms before her feet even touched the ground. 'I'm pretty sure the sea's cold this time of year. Far too cold for a wimpy Englishwoman.'

'You wouldn't dare!' Hannah shrieked.

'Wanna bet?' Jake challenged, and she knew when she was beaten.

'All right. I give in,' she groused half-heartedly. 'It's lovely. All right.'

He put a hand up to his ear. 'You want to repeat that, honey? Not sure I heard it right the first time. Did I hear you say it's the prettiest ring you've ever seen and that I have wonderful taste?'

Hannah sighed. 'Yes you did, and you certainly do. Bully.'

'Good. I'll tell our mothers they did a good job,' he tossed out, giving her another broad smile.

She stared at him, unable to believe she'd heard right. 'They know about this?'

'Yep.' Jake beamed. 'You can ask them yourself if you like.'

His reply clicked through her confused brain, and she stumbled over her words. 'Do you mean to say — '

Jake stuck his hand up in the air and waved it over his head. Hannah glanced over his shoulder and watched in disbelief as their parents stepped out from Jake's kitchen and headed towards them. Mikkel was smiling and carrying a silver tray, which he set down on the table where they'd just finished eating. Hannah could only stare at the bottle of champagne sticking out of a bucket of ice and six crystal glasses. Jake eased her down to standing and wrapped his arm around her shoulders, pulling her close.

'Good news. For some crazy reason she said yes.' Jake's voice cracked on the last word.

'The boy has done something sensible at last.' Mikkel's dry comment was accompanied by a broad grin as he patted Jake on the back. Everyone started to congratulate them at the same time. Her own mother and Elsa both grasped Hannah's hand to inspect the ring.

'Don't act as if you haven't seen it before,' Hannah jibbed. 'I already know someone didn't choose it alone.'

Elsa shuddered. 'You do not want to imagine what you would have ended up with if your dear mother and I had not intervened.'

'The words 'Christmas' and 'cracker' would be involved,' Janie piped up, and in an instant they were all laughing again.

'Have you quite finished mocking me?' Jake said with fake sternness, and

Mikkel chuckled.

'No. This is only the beginning. You will have to get used to it,' he joked, and then his face turned serious. 'You are a lucky man. Never forget that.' He held Elsa's hand. 'I never do.'

Hannah glanced at her own parents, pleased to see her father looking less thin and drawn. She sensed something different between them, but would keep her mouth shut for now. There would be plenty of time to talk later.

'Champagne time, I think,' Jake declared and proceeded to pop open the bottle and pour them each a glass. He passed them around and raised his own glass in the air. '*Skal.* A toast to my beautiful fiancée, and soon-to-be wife.'

'Soon?' Hannah asked.

'Very soon,' Jake replied.

She didn't argue, but raised her glass and met his mesmerizing eyes, which were full of love and happiness. In her head she silently toasted Aunt Betsy and Rose Cottage for bringing her home at last.

We do hope that you have enjoyed reading this large print book.

Did you know that all of our titles are available for purchase?

We publish a wide range of high quality large print books including:
Romances, Mysteries, Classics
General Fiction
Non Fiction and Westerns

Special interest titles available in large print are:
The Little Oxford Dictionary
Music Book, Song Book
Hymn Book, Service Book

Also available from us courtesy of Oxford University Press:
Young Readers' Dictionary
(large print edition)
Young Readers' Thesaurus
(large print edition)

For further information or a free brochure, please contact us at:
Ulverscroft Large Print Books Ltd.,
The Green, Bradgate Road, Anstey,
Leicester, LE7 7FU, England.
Tel: (00 44) **0116 236 4325**
Fax: (00 44) **0116 234 0205**

Other titles in the
Linford Romance Library:

CHRISTMAS IN THE BAY

Jo Bartlett

Maddie Jones runs a bookshop in the beautiful St Nicholas Bay. Devoted to her business, she's forgotten what it's like to have a romantic life — until Ben Cartwright arrives, and reminds her of what she's missing. But Ben isn't being entirely honest about what brings him to town — and when his professional ambition threatens Maddie's livelihood, their relationship seems doomed. When a flash flood descends on the Bay, all the community must pull together — will Ben stay or go?